RED LINE

BY CHARLES BOWDEN

RED LINE

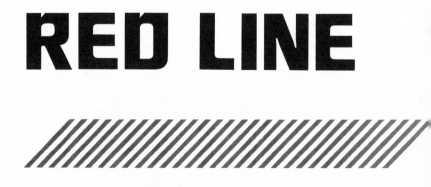

CHARLES BOWDEN

W. W. NORTON & COMPANY
NEW YORK / LONDON

Lyrics on pages 41, 77–78 from "Runaway," written by Del Shannon/Max Crook. © 1961 Mole Hole Music (BMI)/Unichappell Music (BMI). Administered by Bug.
  Lyrics on page 134 from "I Dreamed I Saw St. Augustine," written by Bob Dylan. Copyright 1968 by Dwarf Music. All rights reserved. International copyright secured. Reprinted by permission.

The text of this book is composed in Aster, with display type set in Gamma Bold Extended, Angular Extended. Composition and manufacturing by Haddon Craftsmen Inc.
Book design by Charlotte Staub.

First Edition

Library of Congress Cataloging-in-Publication Data

Bowden, Charles.
  Red Line / Charles Bowden.—1st ed.
    p.   cm.
  "Published simultaneously in Canada by Penguin Books Canada Ltd."—T.p. verso.
  1. Southwest, New—Description and travel—1981–   2. Southwest, New—Social life and customs.   3. Bowden, Charles.   4. Narcotics dealers—Southwest, New.   I. Title.
F787.B69   1989
304.2'0979—dc20   89–8538

ISBN 0-393-02759-7

W. W. Norton & Company, Inc., 500 Fifth Avenue, New York, N. Y. 10110
W. W. Norton & Company Ltd., 37 Great Russell Street, London WC1B 3NU

1 2 3 4 5 6 7 8 9 0

FOR BEN

December 25, 1977—December 19, 1987

A better man than I am.

Your country is desolate, your cities are burned with fire; your land, strangers devour it in your presence, and it is desolate, as overthrown by strangers.

—*Isaiah 1:7*

RED LINE

Things keep banging against my head. For example, there is this letter to Waldo Frank penned in May 1919 by Van Wyck Brooks: "Never believe people who talk to you about the west, Waldo; never forget that it is we New Yorkers and New Englanders who have the monopoly of whatever oxygen there is in the American continent."

I remember making a note of that comment and now for years it has idled in my mind. I make a lot of notes for no real purpose. There is this explosion by Ben Hecht in his memoir, *Child of the Century,* that has dogged me also.

Two generations of Americans have been informed nightly that a woman who betrayed her husband (or a husband his wife) could never find happiness; that sex was no fun without a mother-in-law and a rubber plant around; that women who fornicated just for pleasure ended up as harlots or washerwomen; that any man who was sexually active in his youth later lost the one girl he truly loved; that a man who indulged in sharp practices to get ahead in the world ended up in poverty and with even his own children turning on him . . . that an honest heart must always recover from a train wreck or a score of bullets and win the girl he loved; that the most potent and brilliant of villains are powerless before little children, parish priests, or young virgins with large boobies. . . .

I can never see the stuff coming, I can never figure out any particular place or mood or reason for its arrival. When I was a boy, I imagined an oak-paneled study, the center of the room anchored by a sturdy table with a dull gloss, the walls lined with thick books, many of which, of course, are uniform editions with paper nameplates glued carefully to the spine, and out the study's window, which has small panes of glass, the eye sees that squirrel whirling across the cropped, tired grass of fall. A fine old volume with a silk bookmark rests in my lap, I look up from time to time to contemplate a hard thought or sweet line. Every night dinner is at seven and the wineglass glows on an achingly thin stem, the globe rich with a correct and powerful red. This room is where the messages will come, delivered always in a serif typeface with the footnotes trailing at the bottom of the page in the proper nineteenth-century fashion. But it has not turned out that way, not even the goddamn squirrel moving across the perfectly mown grounds under the ancient, wise trees.

I am riding in a car during a Michigan summer night and we are drunk and a guy in the front seat begins singing,

> Everybody wants to get to heaven,
> But nobody's ready to die.

The cool breath of the lake pours through our hair on the country roads lined with big trees. Without the music, the last few decades would remain political prisoners of the *New York Times.*

As I live, these little bursts of words, and thousands of others, move with me through the small rooms and under the big sky. It is a kind of music playing so softly it never disturbs the conversation, but a music I always half listen to.

Things like Peter the Great scribbling to Catherine, his empress, "But there is only one bottle of vodka left. I don't know what to do."

I'm one up on the Czar. The cheap bottles seem to be in good supply. Still I understand the question of Czar Peter the Great.

I have no ready answer.

Who does?

I walk south two hours, cross the line, and am in Mexico again. The wind whips along the rock mountain while a pale sun bleeds across the February sky. It is 33 degrees. I am wearing shorts, a T-shirt, and a sixty-pound pack. Yesterday I saw an eagle. Today I listen to the cannons of the Air Force playing war over my shoulder on the desert flats of the United States.

I strike Mexican Highway 2 and enter the small café. Out front a yellow dog eats a dead dog. The carcass seems like a mummy as the animal worries the dry hide. I watch his mouth chew the gristle and bone. No one else pays any attention. The wind screams, my skin goes red from the cold. Inside, dead light bulbs stare from the ceiling and a television looks blindly from a corner. There is no electricity, there never has been. There is no water. There never has been. The place is filled with wetbacks crowding around tables to get out of the cold. Soon they will drain their cups of heavily sugared coffee and begin walking north to rumors of work. They smile at my dress, laugh at my pack, and buy me a plate of beans and tortillas.

I have been walking for two hundred miles. I buy a pack of cigarettes, drink the strong coffee, and begin to speak again. They ask me where I have been. I point out into the desert, mumble how many clicks have pounded through the soles of my running shoes. They shake their heads and twirl their fingers to identify the crazy man of the sands, *el loco del desierto.*

There is a broken-down station wagon outside. One man talks with me over coffee and then rises and goes out to where a guy buries himself in the engine with a wrench. The light is so pale—I think this is a café of ghosts. The two men talk and I have a ride.

The car barely moves, the back piled high with boxes of Pampers, kids, the wife, and an old man. The family has been to Mexicali for supplies, they run a small *tienda* in Sonoyta. We stop after three miles, more work under the hood, more transmission fluid poured into the heart of the wounded beast. Everyone smiles and laughs, the cold whips us with a razor tongue. The old man crawls from the back seat, scratches the stubble on his face, and drains a can of Coke. He pitches the empty by the road where it joins a sea of litter.

The trip continues in this halting way. Huge semis scream around us, the horns flaring out with big sounds from the crazed repertoire of the Mexican trucker—the a hooogaa, a hooogaa that slithers across the landscape. I speak my version of Spanglish and everyone tolerates this butchery of language. The desert is flat in this weak light, a pan of creosote punctured here and there by skinny towers of the saguaro. I lift my eyes, see ten men with water jugs going through the fence to *El Norte.* The driver nods toward them and says, *"Mojados,"* the border Spanish word that means wetbacks. I crane my neck, and see the row of white T-shirts melting into the rock and brush.

I think of a field worker I interviewed. A septic field bubbled to the surface near the one-room shack he shared

with four other men, a building left over from the tourist
court heyday of the 1930s. He was twenty-eight years old,
sported a T-shirt celebrating the Los Angeles Olympics,
and he said, "I was born in Guanajuato.

"I came here in 1977.

"I don't go to Mexico.

"I have twelve sisters and brothers in Mexico.

"I am here for the money and the work and the oranges
and the citrus."

It sounded so damn reasonable.

My legs are a patchwork of scars from thorns and
barbed wire. My face is a ruin from the wind and cold. My
eyes are hard crystals that cannot focus on anything after
weeks of drifting carelessly across a landscape where no
one lives and almost no one ever comes to visit. My partner and I split up after two hundred miles of cold camps
and not much talk. A bone in my foot finally gave out, his
desire to finish the journey remained undiminished. He is
now plunging down toward the Sea of Cortes, plodding
sensibly across the great dunes. He will find no one out
there, he will see no sign of our kind, and right now I
suspect he is on his hands and knees inspecting the micro-
flowers that dot the dunes like strange grains of sand. I
will find him in a few days, have a drink and bring him
home. I will say, how was the trip? He will say, fine. And
that will pretty much cover it for both of us.

The broken-down car pulls over in Sonoyta and I buy a
six-pack of Tecate. The cold beer makes us feel warm. The
family is very kind and wishes that my way proves to be
the same as God's way. U.S. Customs is more secular. I
walk up the car lane. The pack excites the eyes of the fat
guy manning the booth.

"What is in there?" he demands. I toss the sixty-pound
sack at him. The thing is encrusted with dirt, rich with the
aromas of weeks out on the ground. My whole body reeks
from a season without a bath. This morning, when I

awoke, the water was frozen. And those days it did not freeze, the jugs were much too precious to squander on personal hygiene. I am a beast and have the scent to prove it. He recoils.

"What is in there? What are you bringing back from Mexico?" he repeats.

"Booze. Dirt."

He scowls and walks away. I am home.

My truck is still safely parked in front of a house. A woman answers the door after a lot of pounding. Her face is flushed, small flecks of sweat gleam from her forehead. She has dressed hurriedly. No, I cannot stay, I say. I hear a man's voice in the other room.

I drive into the late afternoon. The truck moves very slowly at first, I am ill at ease with the velocity of the desert streaming past my windows. The engine seems foreign and menacing. Minute by minute the speedometer creeps up to forty-five. At Why, Arizona, I pull over at a gas station. The small office is full of Indians and the wind bleats against the glass. I buy a six-pack as the night comes down.

The darkness is seldom violated by lights. The Indian villages here are very few and they tend to shelter in the mesquites away from prying eyes. Off to the south in the darkness is a dead village, one abandoned long ago when Apache raids became too much for the people. I know this because once an old man riding in the truck mumbled the story to me. The scholars would like to dig this village up, to bring its bones into the light of day, but the people refuse. They are said to keep a guard on the tomb of their former home. They say if it is dug, the Apache dead will be disturbed. And then, they might come back. I play tapes, the cab rocks with sound. And I drink. A coyote flashes across my headlights, the beer feels rich and foreign as it flows down my throat. A heap of cans begins to build on the floor.

The truck performs poorly—it seems like something in

the fuel line. I do not care. I never care about machines. I punish them without mercy. When I owned a sports car, I rode the red line. It would be late at night and I would be tearing across some state and the tachometer would glow softly in the warm darkness. I would inch the revs up and ride the red line. I wanted to cross it, see if the engine would shoot up through the hood, the cylinders surrender, rods rocketing into the evening stillness. I do not know why. My mechanic hated working on the car. He would look at me with a stony face as if I were a child molester.

I am coming back. I am always leaving and yet I have no home. No one does anymore. We are a nation of homeless people. We have addresses but not homes. And that is why we cannot be travelers. For such a task, you must have a base, a rooted attachment to ground, and then you sally forth and visit the foreign region, note the odd and curious customs, file a report for the folks back home. I read accounts—mainly by bored Englishmen—of journeys into hard deserts, primitive camps, bad food, and no proper tea. They are always womanless and eager for the flagellation of fierce sun or the purge of amoebic dysentery. And no matter where they are, no matter what they are doing, they are always in England. They know how things should be. That is finished, a nineteenth-century kind of thing. We are through with traveling.

But the movement continues and I am typical of this hunger for motion. I take no vacations. I just leave, go, race. I have to leave. The sun bakes me at noon, the night whispers through the fog of wine at midnight. I have to leave.

I drive very fast toward the horizon.

I hoist a pack on my back and walk for days or weeks.

I pedal a bicycle hundreds of miles.

I have to leave.

I can see my need on the faces of people around me. Something is building, the shape of the thing crosses their eyes like a summer storm, and they say, "You should go away." And so I do.

I am dangerous around maps. They beckon me, especially blank spaces. I am very easily frightened but my feelings of fear remain suppressed when I face the orderly universe constructed by cartographers. The house has piles of maps, rolled up, pasted on walls, spilled out on the floors. They are covered with dust, and when I trace a fantasy of motion across them my finger leaves a clean line.

I sometimes go alone. Or with one other person if they will leave me alone. After days of plodding, I find it difficult to talk. I think of women but do not seek them out. And I slow down.

I never carry weapons. I carry money and instant coffee. I think I usually begin by running away from something. Soon I forget what I am fleeing. Actually, I am not too sure about this matter of fleeing, but flight, to speak of flight, is a convention of our time, and so it is easier to shout about escape than to admit or face real motives. When I sleep I do not dream, and when I awaken, I lie on the ground somewhere in the blackness and light my small stove for coffee. The sun rises over the rim of my cup.

Others tell me what I do is odd or foolish.

I envy Stanley seeking Livingstone. He had a reason that the market accepted. I do not know what I am looking for. I wonder if others share these appetites and sensations. But I never ask.

What I want to do is scream that I am weary of concerns, menus, words, fine dinners, and good china plates on good wooden tables. That your homes are clean, your beds soft, your limbs warm and comforting, but this is not enough. That I crave your lips but flee your grip. The music does it to me a lot. Everyone has excellent music, accurate speakers, and makes better coffee than I can. They also favor me with good wine. And at times I love everyone and am incapable of flinging my anger at others.

Then, there are these very quiet incidents that almost shatter my eardrums.

I am leaning against a sofa and a light comedy plays on the VCR. The child crawls at my feet. The air of security and comfort in the room weighs many tons. It is like a drug in a syringe on the table before me. No one else can see the syringe. It is something called imaginary. I reach, pick up the kit, my sleeve rolls up, and the needle aims at a vein. I lust for the drug, can feel the waves of calm washing across my battered cells. But I can't push down the damn plunger.

Or the bar is dark, the MTV safe and sanitary, and the glasses of red wine appear like magic. There is a group, we are talking—ecology, politics, the boredom of eighteenth-century English writing—we are talking and the talk is good. A clock is ticking, no one mentions it or admits its existence, but it is ticking, I can hear its damn ticking. The clock keeps track of the talk so that there will be just enough and so that it will be given at just the right pitch and pace. I sense everyone is remembering a life they never lived. Or would truly want to.

Sometimes it is night and the parking lot is filled and I am standing there with a woman and a car of kids goes past, slows, shouts some bad talk, and goes on. I have had too much to drink but that is not a factor. This a night when drink will never accomplish its proper work. I turn and ask if they'd like to kiss my ass, I suggest they shove their heads up their asses. I am insulting, foolish, pointless, and released into a kind of bliss I seldom find. They drive out of the lot.

It is late at night, jazz plays through Klipsch speakers, and she walks with ease across the room, a room filled with objects that state her and please her. Even the clock is perfect. Her smile, my God that smile, how does she do it? It is as if she knows something I will never fathom. She has curved hips, generous breasts. She is a nineteenth-century body waiting patiently through the anorexic times.

She says, "Relax."

She means it, she truly means it.

Nothing seems wrong. But I still go.

Often these flights are disguised with the garments of business. This is always a lie. For years now I have had the same experience: I am working, sitting in a chair, the electric lights playing across my table or desk. I feel the bones snapping in my body and think my entire life at the moment is safe, useless, and like many another. I sense that I can manage, if I mind my manners, to squander all my days and nights and die in bed confirming what I never believed. And that this act will win approval. From everyone, including me. I see myself dead, properly dead. Perhaps, kind lies are being said about me. My bones are snapping.

Temptations constantly flash across my mind. I have no control over this matter, nor have I sought such control. I see a flat of greasewood and the light is white, the air is still with the furnace breath of noon. When I listen hard, the hearts beating in the doves murmur against my ears. The ground bears no tracks of human beings and all the leaves on the huddled mesquites and ironwoods are a gray-green with dust and fatigue. There are mountains, always there are mountains, printed like a brown smudge against the horizon line. I enter this frame. At my foot is the skull of a kangaroo rat, the lobes huge, the surface smooth and finely wrought. A man once told me you can always tell the bone of a man. Your tongue will stick, he said. I do not know if this fact is true. I simply want to believe it. I walk into the frame, pick up the skull of rat, and lick. My ambitions are very old and simple and almost always unvoiced. I want to be whole. I do not know what this condition would feel like and there is no advice on the matter that convinces me. I am not sure exactly what whole means and, to be honest, it sounds too much like being finished.

Late at night, I like to sit in a darkened room with just

one small light, the wattage very low, and look at the re-flections on the window. My face then bounces back as a faint, ghostly thing. This strikes me as the way we move through life, spectral forms drifting across the strong waters, hard ground, and spikes of sound that rise up from the floor of appetite. The planet spins through the cold sky. We drift by. I do not wish to remain such a ghost. So I enter the frame. I am sure there are words to dismiss this act and this ambition. I am very good at coining words for dismissing such behavior.

I must meet someone for supper or drinks in an hour or two. I keep my engagement and over the drink I say I am leaving. Maps spill out onto the table, my finger races here and there and here. I spin a trajectory of logic, a journey that makes perfect sense. This part is always a lie. But it temporarily convinces, like a painkiller that will not wear off for days or hours. The comments are always the same.

"When will you be back? Is it safe? You're sure you're going to be okay?"

Of course, of course, I purr, it is simple, actually almost boring in its ordinariness. It is just a quirk of my nature—I must see this place, I must taste this experience, I must visit this historic site. I must go. I do not speak of the skull of the kangaroo rat or the feel of the bone against my tongue.

She says, "I must buy you dinner. We must make a real occasion of it."

A fine bottle of wine appears, we grow very soft and affectionate. The food is very rich, the view from the window quite good—twinkling city lights abstracting a behavioral sink into form and color. And then we part.

But first she always says the same thing, regardless of who she is: "You're crazy."

Perhaps.

NACHO

My son is born at first light. The body is slippery, the head covered with dark hair. The labor has been ten hours. I have come to the hospital straight from work on a Saturday night. There is no marriage surrounding this event, we do not live together, there has been no careful plan. These words sound in my ears like a grocery list of failure. I am forty-one years old and now I am beginning a life when my own feels like a last chapter. I have been sitting at my office in a room where the windows cannot be opened and for days I have been checking spellings, glancing at layouts, writing headlines, scratching out teases for the cover of the magazine. There has been little sleep, but then sleeplessness has been a fact for about two years. Publications, like wars, are sacred causes. Then the phone rings, she says the moment has arrived, and I go. This is no way to live, they tell me.

The hospital chills me, such encampments always do. The walls and faces shout, Watch out! You might slip on a banana peel! This is the American zone of caution, injury, and fear. I think, what a place to begin life, in a huge building devoted to proving life is hardly worth all the risks. All the wings are named for crushed Indian tribes. I hold the baby in a room of cool tiles while three doctors look up from the surgical table ever so briefly to see if the bond has taken. I walk down an empty hall and into a sterile room where I place my son on a scale like a sack of flour. He is four minutes old and now the numbers begin for him. I am very tired and feel no resistance as the DNA whips around me like steel cables and lashes me to a future that seems to have no end or beginning. I return to the operating theater. There is the slightest pause, then the three men sink back into the busy work of their knives and needles.

I go home, sleep briefly, return to work. And then at dusk, I drive toward a bosque of mesquite against the mountain. It is the graduation ceremony of an institute where people gather to study nature and the death of nature so that they will become calm warriors in the battles of a war called environmental. Such warriors are always well bred, courteous, and garbed in quiet tones of the earth. The men often have beards, but trimmed beards, the women wear pants, but not tight pants. Behind us the mountain looms, a pile of stone that we call an intricate ecology in the hope that we can cage it with language. But tonight, as a storm licks at its peaks, the mountain is the very thing that filled our ancestors with fear, the hellish temple where gods roamed, beasts dominated, and devils perched on ledges waiting for our red blood and soft flesh. The crowd spreads out under the trees and I begin to speak as thunder rumbles, gusts of wind sweep through, and small stabs of lightning lance the paling sky. I tell them of sierras, of long walks, the value of the thing we call nature or Nature. I am dead on my feet but I manage to struggle through a litany of injuries inflicted on the land and ourselves. I am what they bought, the prophet of all our bad ways. And those ways are inscribed on my face and burned into my eyes. I am also the wanderer who has begat a child. I stand there prattling but what I think of is a quote from Sterne that booms all a man can do is begat a child, build a house, write a book, plant a tree. I have done three of the four and it is not enough.

Afterwards I drink wine and talk with the people. They are very concerned about the environment. And I agree. But somehow my notion of the term is more elastic and covers things others never want seen in the light of day. Of course, in my talk I skirted this fact. It would be unseemly to discuss such ideas. But they fester within me. When I love the gleam in a lion's eyes as it glares into my flashlight in the heavy hours of the night, I feel the same overwhelming sense of agreement that seizes me when I watch a developer flip a deal and butcher a thousand acres, listen over beers to a fighter pilot describe scorching the calm of the planet as he drops his jet down to the desert floor at that speed we believe escapes sound. I have never found a walk across an empty valley and over the hard rock of an isolated sierra that can kill within me the need to drive a car as fast as possible through a soft summer night. My audience under the fine gnarled mesquite trees against the big mountain, they love the form of the lion moving as a flowing yellow ghost across the perfect landscape. But I also love the teeth, the sharp, tearing teeth, the jaws opened wide and driving the life out of the deer's neck. The warm blood flooding the tongue of the beast. But I share with them the hope that life is based on reason and that good people can gradually fashion a good planet. I even half believe this. I tell them we are hacking the land to death but somehow the land will yet save us. Then I drive my truck to the hospital so that I can hold my son. When I reach the hospital room, it is vacant. When I press my nose against the glass of the nursery, the crib is empty. I run down the corridors, flying past nurses and patients. It turns out to be a simple thing, a slight fever, a few hours in the intensive-care ward. But I cannot forget the feeling, that violent rise of fear and anger, the fists forming in my hands. I have been put on notice, something in me has changed, or if not changed, has been revived. I go to bed at dawn.

That morning a passing motorist notices the bodies in the tall grass west of town. They are out in the open, two men, hands tied behind their backs, bullets pumped into their heads. It is Monday, April 27, 1987, and the sun is brilliant in Tucson. The day will be hot. The two men have been dead a few hours, my son has been alive twenty-four. I remember the weather.

Arturo Carrillo Strong comes to my office clutching small clips from the newspaper. The dead have been identified and dismissed. Art is fifty-seven, an ex-narc now retired. But actually, he is more than a century old, perhaps a century and a half old. His people have been in this town about that long, and in the surrounding desert their presence runs so deep that not even folk tales can recall their arrival. Public buildings bear the Carrillo name. He is grounded into something I cannot join, a gnarled, twisting thing, like the root of a mesquite probing the hot ground and then plunging deeper and deeper into the heart of the desert seeking that taste of water that will temporarily kill the thirst that is driving it mad with need. Once in a mine south of town, they found a living mesquite root twitching with lust more than 150 feet beneath the surface of things. Art is always smiling on his surface, but beneath the flash of his teeth, the hearty rumble in his throat, deeper and darker, is this brooding, a hard yet soft feeling that glares nakedly from his eyes. He is a man who has never been fully fed. None of his adventures has been enough, none of the collars, none of the wild nights and the careless bottles tossed aside under a desert moon, none of these things has been enough. He is still so terribly hungry. He prowls, he probes, he listens, he haunts places. He has excuses for these acts—he is the ex-cop hooked on cop ways, he is the son of the ancient family interested in local history, he is the child of the barrio anxious to stay in touch, he is friendly guy in the bar ready for a good time at seven in the morning. But he is simply hungry for a taste of real goods, for the sharp slice of the edge, for the darker moments when the desert blazes with a strange light. We were made for each other.

The word on the street, he tells me, is that men met a drug deal that went bad. One of them, a *cholo* named Ignacio Robles Valencia, has a big rep as a killer. The other man is his cousin, Carlos Enrique Lopez.

The rosary for Lopez is packed with local heavyweights in the drug business. Flowers flood the room with scent, there is the odor of smelling salts knifing through this floral haze. Women weep. The casket is of the finest grade of wood and stern-faced young men stand at the head and foot of the coffin and scan the crowd. Outside, the parking lot chokes on four-wheel-drive Chevy trucks complete with oversized tires, roll bars, fancy lights, and tons of chrome. Three machines are required to carry the floral displays to the gravesite. Ignacio Robles Valencia rides to eternity in the same style. The casket is again of the finest grade, the body dressed in new Levis and a new cowboy shirt. The family comes up from Nogales, Sonora, sixty miles away, to bring his remains back home. Antonio, Ignacio's younger half brother, appears to be very much in command. He wears a colorful western shirt with gold lapel ornaments and highly polished cowboy boots. Around his waist is a fancy leather belt with a large, round, silver and gold buckle concealing a small derringer that can be detached instantly. The body is loaded into the funeral coach and the small caravan prepares to leave. There is the matter of the bill—a sum of $1,500 paid in full with tens and twenties. I know these facts because Art's people have handled the Mexican dead of this city for generations.

The hair is silver, the beard clipped close. His hearing is shot in one ear. He is half Anglo but seems to regret this fact. His core is *Mejicano* and he is full of smiles, jokes, and hard, dark angers. He is that thing called a Mexican American, a man immersed in the Anglo world and yet tied by some cord I can never quite see to whispers and incantations of a lost continent of Latinos. I have lived here most of my life and Art is the man I often meet, the border person who can talk my language but never think my thoughts—or want to.

We all think we are Americans, and we are. But neither of us knows what this means. Art and I are constantly finding common ground—football scores, old dives, favored drinks, the strong links of American consumerism. And then in a split second—the cry of a baby, the gesture of a woman, the crackle of a story on the radio—in these tiny instants, our common ground will fall apart and we will become two islands facing each other across a forbidding sea. I will walk away from family instantly and call this desertion work. Art finds this inconceivable.

We are both riding in Art's truck, we have been on the south side of town, perhaps, talking to the rough boys. They have poured us drinks, I have drained glasses of burgundy and Art has tossed down shots of Seagram Seven, and Art is talking to a brown man in gold chains and the man is professing to not know English—a lie we mutually ignore—and I am professing to be totally ignorant of Spanish, and afterward as we walk out, Art and I will confer as to what it all meant, what was really going on. (Did you notice the gun, the ring, the flicker of the eye toward the other man, the pistoleros off to the side? What, you did not see them? Shit, I begin to wonder about you gringos, you didn't notice the gun held between their legs? Shit.) Anyway, we are riding and I am talking and I say something and Art looks over with absolute pity and says, "Don't you ever stop analyzing things? Don't you ever stop thinking?" And I know what he means and I have no answer. Because I know the answer. So I sit in the Mexican bars and drink and listen to the music. And think.

Art does not analyze. He does not think about what he is doing. He has a defense for his actions: Nacho is a case, he is the ex-cop who cannot cease being a cop. He is working up the facts, getting ready to make the collar. None of this is true, but it is enough for people, and so he does not have to address his hungers in public. But there is an anger in his eyes, almost a fury, that cannot be explained by simply saying police work, old habits of the trade. He is hunting not the crimes of Nacho, but the force, the thing that blasted him out of the barrio and into our lives. When Art was a boy, his grandfather would pay other boys in the barrio to fight him so that his grandson would become hard. Art now laughs about this memory. But he remembers.

At the office, I am beginning to slip, people around me speak of me as a kind of dead person, as someone who is "off the rails." Naturally, I disagree. I feel something going on but think they miss what it is. My mind is foraging, slipping from my control or direction. I do not daydream, I do not dream. I drift. My mind roams. Words, faces, scents, fragments of things appear suddenly. I am talking to someone, and I drift off. But not off the rails. Just off. A statement, a memory, a string of words. Off.

> *At the present rate of progression, since 1600, it will not need another century or half century to tip thought upside down. Law in that case would disappear as a theory . . . and give way to force. Morality would become police. Explosives would reach cosmic violence. Disintegration would overcome integration.*
> *—Henry Adams,*
> *A Letter to American Teachers of History, 1910*

We decide to ask questions. I still do not know why. No one on earth wants this story. It is the classic who-cares feature. A psychopathic killer is bad enough, a Mexican is worse, a Mexican national worse yet. I am in a business and this tale cannot be sold. Look at any newspaper and a killing on the Mexican end of town is page twelve, a shot fired at a kid on a skateboard in the good neighborhoods is page one. But I am possessed. I see something in the fabric of killing and hunger and drugs and dark streets that beckons. Some can survive on solid wages, clean homes, the good woman, the children, and sure, safe routines. I cannot and I do not approve of this fact. It is as if in spite of my every conscious desire, something takes over in me, something flaming out of my humdrum self. My fingers rub up and down along the edges of the small newspaper clipping. It is a passage from a Talmud, a new Rosetta Stone, and if I can decipher it, parse out the strange glyphs, fathom the odd metaphors, I will know. I will have less to learn. I will not be as hungry.

I am going after Nacho because . . . that is the question written on the faces of the people around me. I am an editor and editors sit at desks, take long lunches, ride herd on unruly sentences and revive stories that are flooded with language but missing an engine to make them move. I walk the hall of the magazine, the fluorescent lights bearing down with their drizzle of pallor, the busy faces of my co-workers plotting new features, notices for plays and ballets, reviews of fine restaurants, profiles of local officeholders, I am padding down that long corridor and I have this serial killer splattered all over my body. I stand at the coffeemaker and pour from a glass pot into a styrofoam cup, the moment seems so clean and exact. People laugh around me, smiles flash, the women are well dressed, the men well rested, and I smell the coffee and catch a whiff off the bodies lying by the roadside in the dawn of an April day.

I am going after Nacho because I am as hungry and empty as he is. The details of my life have begun to catch up with me. The marriage blew off the table almost half a decade ago, just blew off the table like a paper plate at a picnic. And I have never bothered to retrieve it. The separation has become enduring, the divorce some magical legal world that stays just beyond my reach. The women seem to come in squads without pattern or plan. And then, of course, the child, the mother of the child, both facts, unbeckoned but facts I cannot deny or let go of or even regret. But facts that seem secondary to a dead man who liked to kill people. I operate in a world of words, piles of copy, phone calls from printers, hard deadlines, a maze called a distribution system, racks of magazines booming at shoppers in checkout lines. The business meetings are endless, long sessions where the obvious is dissected, the numbers seized upon or ignored, the table lined with pale faces, their eyes dull like those of a dried cod. I work eighty to one hundred hours a week and when the day ends, the night begins, dark evenings drinking with developers as they denounce rules and plan their weekend at the beach on the coast, numbing sessions with politicians who always smile and peer out from hooded eyes, the cocktail parties with platters of rich snacks and women beaming from fine dresses that slip so easily from their bodies. When I get home, the house is a maze of cobwebs, the bills pile up on the table, the meals are infrequent and cold, the bottles lie about the floor like abandoned lovers. My life is a heap of phone messages neatly recorded on pink slips, messages seldom answered. In the morning, I get up before dawn, fall into my truck, and as I drive the clogged streets I keep my eyes locked on the roadway so that I will not see the faces of people at the bus stops. If I falter, and catch a glimpse of the fatigue and anger and dreams floating on their eyes, I will pull over and get out and walk away.

I realize that I have somehow done the one thing I had not foreseen would drain me of blood and leave me a body without heat or lusts, leave me a corporate man. I have left the streets and now life is leaving me. The women are another matter. The emptier I become, the more important their flesh is to me. They are all very tender, warm, and intelligent. And random. Out of this barrenness the child comes like an unexpected summer rain. I go past the coffeemaker, down the long corridor, out the door and into the barrio looking for a dead man who murdered men, women, and children because I know this will restore me to life. I have been a student of hunger and now I decide to feed. I do not care about the table setting, I eye the knife.

The dead exist in fragments. I am in the newsroom of *La Voz del Norte*, the newspaper of Nogales, Sonora. The editor sits at a clean desk, a small radio on the shelf behind him.

"Ignacio Robles? Nachito? Yes, we knew of him. Why do you ask?"

It always begins this way—Gringo, why now do you suddenly want to know? There is no real answer. I flourish a business card, his brown hand reaches out, examines the small rectangle like it is a profound document. Art is babbling away in Spanish, he is Arturo Carrillo now, forget the Strong, he is the *hombre*, perhaps, if you give the slightest opening, the *campañero*. The room floods with light from the roar of the June sun, there is very little going, not even the tap of a typewriter. Mexican women, slightly overweight and in tight skirts, sit in the outer office at old Royals. Their faces are very made up and they look all business. But their eyes give them away, the eyes are nesting in dark wells of color with hints of turquoise and the eyes flash with sweaty desires. The quality of the newsroom is quite different from the United States. Here the government controls the paper supply and if you decide to print what you want, well, then you get no paper. This makes the work quite easy.

A man is sent, a big, strong-looking man with gold chains, and he returns with the paper of the day after the killings. In the States, the two bodies slipped away as small change and a few blurted inches of type. Here, the headline screams: ASSASSINATION OF "NACHITO" ROBLES IN TUCSON. THE END OF THE DANGEROUS MULTIPLE MURDERER.

The Spanish tortures my brain as I plunge into a loose translation: At the beginning of this year, Nachito Robles had occasion to be released from jail by the authorities for a homicide in which he had presumably stabbed a young man during a fiesta in the Colonia Heroes. If one takes into account his short life, he had resided as a prisoner for many years in the prison of this frontier where he once escaped after killing a guard with a pointed weapon, fleeing into Arizona. And on that occasion, he also killed a police officer. He returned to the border and committed another crime—the kind of thing his life was dedicated to during the sixteen years of his constant activity and his involvement in the "business of murder." Some of his family remember that Nachito was dangerous, and possibly his violent death results from revenge or is mixed up with the business of the narcotics traffic. Police circles indicate that the death of Nachito closes one of the darkest pages of Nogales.

I look up at the editor, his face is all seriousness. I ask, where can I learn more about this Nachito? He recommends we visit another newspaper, one now closed, but one where the old files are rich with the exploits of *El Famoso*. Thank you very much, we say in Spanish, and the man scribbles down the address and name of the publication. We look at it, the rag was the vehicle of a local drug gang, one Nacho did stints of labor for from time to time. Thanks, but no thanks.

The editor promises to send me yet more stories from

his own archive. I offer to pay, but, no! no! Señor, that is not necessary, this is my pleasure. Of course, the clips will never be mailed.

We drive around town. The prison flits past, a modern, grim little fortress with guys in Levis strolling about holding AR-15s. Obregon, the main drag, is clogged with people and machines. We go into the Supermercado so that Arturo can buy some coffee for his wife. The Mexicans drink a stronger brew, one that shames the dishwater tastes of Americans. Across the street is an old cantina, one Arturo remembers from his youth, we must stop in and have a memorial drink or two. It is about noon.

The bar is very dark and full of idle men, mainly young. They sit in small groups talking about the news around town. We are the only gringos, objects of curiosity, perhaps potential resources. Art talks about a ball game now decades dead, a mighty contest in which he and some guys from Tucson came down and played the Nogales guys. The trick was to play hard and lose. If you won, the police escorted you out of town, pronto. If you lost, the winning team took you to this bar and there were drinks on the house, women, all manner of courtesies. I drain my Tecate and feel the hard eyes boring into my back. I sense we have yet to lose the game.

Art rises and goes to the head. A young *cholo* from another table leaps up and follows him in. He asks him if he wants drugs.

The television booms with American baseball. Everyone keeps drinking. The day is barely begun in Nogales. The table is small, like those tiny round ones found in thirties cocktail lounges, and the beer is barely cold. Flies crawl across my body. We have another round. No one speaks to us but they have enormous ears. The noise of trucks rolling down Obregon punches through the saloon walls. Mufflers are a hit-and-miss thing here. We leave, and as we walk out the voices stop, the eyes stare. We make no sense here, and it is bootless to explain our business.

We move a mile down the street to another bar, a fancier place in a big hotel that features off-track betting. There are no other customers. The bartender speaks English, but, of course, will not acknowledge the language. We ask him about Nacho, did he know of such a man? Oh, yes, he says, you can find out about Nacho in any saloon in Nogales.

"El Nacho? Oh, sure, I knew him, I know his father. When Nacho got out of prison about ten years ago, he was sixteen or seventeen, and he came walking up Obregon one night and some kids were burning a tire about block from here in front of the Palace of Justice. It was winter and they were trying to stay warm. My cousin Enrique was there and Nacho said something to him, and then Enrique said something to Nacho, and then Nacho pulled out a screwdriver and drove it through his throat and he died like that. Nacho ran away."

He is rolling now, the words come easily, he is eager to tell the Americanos about the real life of the streets. After all, he is the bartender, the man who lives by stories. Just then his manager comes in and sits at the end of the bar. He is fat, and he listens hard. The barest flicker of a signal comes from his hand, the bartender walks over to him, puts his head down, nods, and then returns. Only now he polishes glasses and when we ask him questions, he is mute. The drinks are starting to rush through my mind, I have not eaten, and I can tell this will be a long, blurry day.

The manager leaves briefly for the head. We lean forward and ask one more question. Where did Nacho live?

"Ah," the bartender whispers, "in the Colonia Buenos Aires, just east of here and behind the hill."

"Is it a rough neighborhood?"

"The Buenos Aires District? Oh, you can go in it. The

police are there during the day. They leave at dark. Just get out before dark."

He laughs softly.

Outside, we pass a news vendor and I buy a small local publication, *Tribuna Regional.* A tiny item explains, "This youth was assaulted by hoodlums in the vicinity of the registered area called Buenos Aires, the worst slum in the city—where we have noticed there is a protection racket against the citizens by the city police."

Elvira's sits by the fence, a restaurant favored by Americans because it serves free tequila with its food. The owner keeps pouring and then an older man, a gray-haired fellow in his sixties, joins us. He is a reporter on the daily paper. The tequila now comes in volume, shot after shot. We must prove we are men. My head reels. Food appears, on the house, we are the guests, the visiting gringos, the *periodistas,* potential *compañeros.* Gingerly, we ask about Nachito. Already we know bits and pieces from talk on the street in Tucson. There is a soft purr in the barrios there about this recent dead man. The résumé is short and crisp: he robbed people, sold dope, and killed people. The tallies on the killings vary—six people, ten people, fifteen people, twenty-eight people, thirty-eight people, sixty people. No one is sure. They all agree on one detail. Nacho killed with a screwdriver, a scissors, or a knife.

The reporter is very happy now, he has worked all day and has a fresh newspaper under his arm. Partly he works for the local Chamber of Commerce drumming up more tourism. The rest of the time he wanders the city gathering tidbits. His face is fat and red, and he wheezes as he speaks.

"El Nacho? Yes, I knew of him and I know his father and mother, too. Killings? I think Nacho did maybe ten in Nogales, perhaps three in Tucson, and somewhere in Arizona they say he killed a cop. When he would escape from prison and kill someone, he would call the police from

Buenos Aires and say, come and get me. He killed at least one cop in this manner. How many did he kill in all? Who knows? In Nogales itself, I think there have been maybe one hundred forty murders in the last six months."

He eats fiercely at the chicken tacos, smacking his lips.

As I walk along I wonder what went wrong
With our love, a love that was so strong.
And as I still walk on I think of the things we've done
Together, while our hearts were young.
                    —"Runaway," Del Shannon

I want to know what it is like to believe in a future. I am waiting with a friend for sunset in Yuma, Arizona, and then we will walk to Palm Springs loosely following the path of the '49ers who crossed the desert with dreams of gold. More than a century ago an army of people poured through Tucson and the Southwest lusting for the gold of California. What they made, we will walk through. We will be lovers moving through the ruins.

That is the soft thought that travels with me. But the hard thought is escape from something that is consuming me. For a week I have been in the barrios tracking Nacho. My body is giving out from the drinking and something else is breaking up, something I cannot yet name, but I feel it falling apart within me. For a week, I have been out before dawn and returning, if at all, in the midnight hour. I have Nacho's portraits on my office wall—the child at thirteen with jail-cell numbers dangling from a plaque around his neck, the blank stare of a crazed hunger artist at twenty-seven. The trip to Yuma was like a fever, me lying in the back of a truck tossing and turning, images stomping across my face. So I have designed a respite, a quick 150- or 200-mile walk across the summer flame of the desert. I will discover nature, drop in on rural society, relax, not look over my shoulder.

We have full packs—candy bars, sardines with jalapenos, sunflower seeds, raisins—and two and a half gallons of water apiece. We're decked out in running shoes, shorts, T-shirts, and caps. An hour ago an Arizona highway patrolman warned us of the danger. He said the wets die coming north, he said now and then he finds old folks along the road dead in their cars, poleaxed by the heat. This is the New West, the place where walking is a suicidal act. It is 6:00 P.M. and 110 in the shade.

The Colorado purrs along a block away and down by the river Benjamin Butler Harris, age twenty-four, rests with fifty-one fellow Texans. He lives in a book, an old journal kept during the Gold Rush, and I have this paperback tucked into my backpack. I was sitting in the dark of my office in Tucson when a call came from the San Francisco *Examiner*. We cut a deal, one manufactured on the spot. I will write, the photographer will snap pictures. And now I will walk from Yuma to Palm Springs tracking the ghost of Benjamin Butler Harris and his kind. It is the summer of 1849 in his camp. Word of the gold strike at Sutter's Mill reached Washington, D.C., on December 7, 1848, and Harris and his friends saddle up and leave Plano, Texas, on March 25, 1849.

He is a lawyer from Tennessee. The men in his party come from just about every state in the Union and several foreign countries. Harris is a dreamer in a nation of dreamers.

Across the river, the Yumas now wait out the United States on a reservation. A century ago, they were a renowned warrior tribe, a tall people who carried war clubs and brained unwelcome visitors. In 1849, twelve thousand men crossed the river here and went for the gold—half Americans, half Sonorans. Harris detests the Yumas. They steal, they charge a high price for crossing the river, and if you lose that half step, they kill you.

When his group left Texas, an old frontiersman gave the pilgrims a bit of advice: "Shoot at every Indian you see and save them a life of misery in subsisting on snakes, lizards, skunks, and other disgusting objects." Now the Yumas steal Harris's favorite mule—the tribe loves to eat them. A huge party comes up and threatens to kill every white man at the crossing. The Texans blow a couple away and things calm down.

I lean against the new Yuma jail and over my head a camera sweeps the grounds for possible menace. The machine grinds as it chews the shadows of our flesh. Mexican women traipse by with their kids in tow, they have come for a visit with the old man. Male eyes burn through the tinted slit windows. It is the night of the Fourth of July and liberty hangs in the hot air. The woman and kids are all brown and I know the eyes behind the windows are black. Soon fireworks will pock the sky and wets will look up as they head north. They will standing in the desert, perhaps pissing on a creosote, and they will marvel at the antics of the *Norte Americanos*.

A year ago, I beached a canoe on the Sea of Cortes and headed north. It was Easter Sunday. In Sonora, every irrigation ditch was lined with people having picnics and the green waters splashed with naked kids shouting into the steaming air. At the border, the silence fell like a police squad and miles of deserted fields rolled past in perfect order. I stopped in a lonely bar and when I drank, the only sound was the whirr of the air conditioner. I was grateful for the quiet and embarrassed for my country.

I want to taste the sensation of dreams and walk with the dreamers. I was born in a fat land starved with wants.

We stand, throw the packs on our shoulders, and move into the sun. It falls like a hammer on our shoulders. The bridge is empty and we amble across the river. Two Mexicans, illegals, slip through the tamarisk below, in their hands plastic milk jugs full of water. They wear straw hats and do not look up.

A little ways upstream thirteen grubby trappers squat on the far bank, their long black powder rifles lean against the trees. They are the lords of this nineteenth-century West, men who glide easily through this desert. A Yuma wrapped in a blanket sidles up to their camp, squats over a trapper's ammunition, and then slips off with his booty. The trapper waits and when the Indian is about seventy yards away brings his rifle up and cuts him down. He walks over, recovers his ammunition, scalps the dead man, and then cuts a strip of skin about twenty inches long from the body. He will use it as a razor strop. One of his companions asks just what he thinks he is doing. He says, "I'm administering on this Indian's estate."

We camp on the bajada above the river, a pudding of bare soil with creosote bushes here and there. I eat a can of sardines. Harris and his friends are down to parched corn, supposed to be the feed for their mules, and nervous about the desert ahead. Harris cannot walk, he has been crippled the entire trip by his own foolishness. Before leaving Texas he danced for three days and when the journey started he could not walk because of his injured toes. They have never healed and so he rides.

We hit the freeway, Interstate 8, and follow along. The culverts under the big road are rich with artifacts: hundreds of human footprints heading north, big empty cups of 7-11's Super Big Gulp. Here and there erupt the tire tracks of the Border Patrol, then the machine stops, and huge American footprints briefly join the legion of feet walking into *El Norte*. The American impressions stand for the rules, black coffee, and endless forms. The Mexicans stand for the appetites. Benjamin Harris is puzzled by the freeways thick with cops; he feels the journey of the Mexicans in his guts. He works through a different world, one rich with space. I must be the good scout finding tiny islands of this world amid the big roads, towns, and flat green fields.

The inspectors peer under cars with mirrors on long metal wands as they search for Gypsy moths. A few yards away a brown nation is scuttling north into the white heat. The state employees in their crisp uniforms have replaced the Yumas as the new gatekeepers in these parts.

I lean against the wall of a neighboring state truck scale, one closed for the day. Flies crawl across my face and I read a Raymond Chandler novel about a lost Los Angeles, one now entombed by freeways. The book fails me in this heat. All the colors on the page are bleached, the women wear scent but cannot sweat, and the entire city sags with weariness toward a big sleep. Chandler's hard cases jabber away. One cracks, "About a year or so back we had him in the cooler on a Mann Act rap. It seems he run Sternwood's hotcha daughter, the young one, off to Yuma." The big sleep slides into the big flight for just a second. I can't remember his city. The one I have brushed against is somehow different. I am twenty and standing by the furnace of a steel mill just east of L.A. The man monitoring the oven turns to me, opens a tiny slot for viewing, and I inch forward. Inside, I see slabs of metal. And a turkey, roasting ever so slowly, for the lunch ahead. I turn back to the big sleep but it is no good. I am visiting L.A. in the seventies and get up in the morning with a hangover and walk to the bathroom. The door is open and the host, a woman, is sitting, applying makeup. She is naked, the hips spreading out soft on the bench, the breasts hanging pale and relaxed. I appear in the mirror behind her. No reaction flickers across her perfect face. I stand there for a moment and then leave. No one ever speaks, ever. It is not necessary.

A few yards off traffic roars back and forth across the continent. In my hands the endless big sleep. I sip water, chew granola bars, swat flies, and read on about the fatigue that has sapped the drive of my culture.

I make notes to salvage the time. But I cannot bear it and get up and walk over to the fruit inspection station. Two women stalk embargoed plants. One lady has wonderfully long red nails and they flash in the air as she motions and then probes the vehicles. She asks me where I am headed with my backpack and I explain the journey.

"There's nothing out there," she sighs, "but farms and then desert."

Yes.

I look down at the ground and see a certificate blowing in the breeze: "California's Inspection Stations Are Its First Line of Defense in Protecting the State's Environment from Destructive Pests."

Yes.

Walter Andres, fifty-eight, has been at the work for thirty-nine years and plans to plug along until his fiftieth wedding anniversary, July 13, 1999. He was born in Yuma and cannot understand people who move around. He is a heavy man and red-faced as he stands at a sink cutting up fruit in his quest for sinister invaders. The voice is weary with the foolishness of life. He looks at me askance—I have no niche in his world. I am on foot by choice.

"You're going to walk north to Glamis?" he says with alarm and he eyes my running shoes with horror. "How much water are you carrying? You gotta have at least five gallons a man a day in this desert. No boots? You need high top boots, though if you hit a sidewinder it won't make much difference. The wets come through here all the time, and they know walking, and they die out there in the desert and nobody finds them for a year and nobody even knows who they were and nobody in Mexico even knows they're missing."

He's got my number, I've lately become a student of finding people in Mexico. He is happy right now, preaching to the laity, burying my preposterous form with the fine dust of his desert expertise. Now that Americans have abandoned the country, have retreated to safe vantage points, they resent anyone who goes out there, or down there, or in there. They wish it all to stay contained in the bell jar of the past.

"You know those folks in '49? Why do you suppose they were out there? It's hard to figure out."

It is a fair question. Walter Andres sits for decades waiting for bad bugs in his small booth and all around him are the ghosts of '49ers and all around him are Americans roaring east and west on the Interstate and all around him are Mexicans marching north into the desert looking for day labor. I tell him it's the gold, they go for the gold.

But I do not believe this.

They go for the dreams.

We leave at dusk and head north toward Glamis, a town of thirteen people wedged against the Algodones dunes. The ground is small, hard, varnished rocks—desert pavement—and littered with one-gallon plastic milk jugs, the basic survival gear of Mexicans. Some have twine tied at the handle. We are in a major corridor for human beings heading toward the work of the Central Valley and the fields at Salinas. They are all around us, keeping out of sight, moving like ghosts in the twilight.

A Border Patrol truck roars up. It is following the dirt path along the railroad track and drags tires to make a clean slate for detecting human footprints later on in the night. The driver appraises us with hunter's eyes—in back are two Mexicans, caged, who gamely wave. He is your basic Border Patrolman—the gunbelt, the pressed uniform, the armor of authority and the small-town air of a man who has escaped a county sheriff's department for a federal paycheck.

He is also annoyed to have us in his desert. This is the basic experience if you are on foot: you are violating everyone's fantasies of the danger waiting out there in the sands and thorns and loneliness. You are ripping away the fabric of their West, the one that requires dune buggies, 4×4s, dirt bikes, sidearms, rifles, long hip knives, stout boots, flares, huge water cans, snakebite kits, salt tablets, curious bonnets, large belt buckles, radios as armor against the teeming populations of poisonous insects eager to stab your hide, the lonely flats anxious for bodies, the strangers who might drift over the horizon and kill you. Americans hate their deserts and consider them useful only for exercises in assault. They are places to shoot holes in cactus, slaughter tortoises, toss beer bottles, tear up hillsides with machines, settle drug deals, leave bullet-riddled bodies in the arroyo, they are places to make fires, places to curse the darkness. The hot, dry ground is the woman—the bitch, slut, whore—who must be beaten, raped, and crushed. This is of course denied, we all feel foolish when we drift into this male/female approach to our hatred of the earth, instead the deserts are called fragile by everyone and many testify how they love the dry air and appreciate the lack of snow. But our actions are inscribed all over the valleys and dunes and I can smell our anger rising off the land.

We cannot face the West we found or the West we sacked. It is all in the photographs. I am on the coast and I am walking through the Museum of Photographic Art in San Diego. The exhibit offers two centuries, the nineteenth and our own. Cameras eat the terrain. The artists are going to make the flesh and blood simple for us. It is all there in black and white. Outside the walls, Balboa Park is full of lush growth, flowers, and bird song. In here with the white walls and clean frames, the world is mainly prints of mountains and deserts and big rocks and huge trees. The frames are a big factor, they are the fat fists of the curator holding the images like icons and insisting that we fire up our minds but kill our loins and study arrangement, aesthetics, tone, and texture. Vistas drip down the walls, rectangles cage the terrain and temper it into form and light and shadow. The planet was created in those six arduous days simply to model for a lens. The dry ground feels the knife, winces, and is anointed art. People drift by, talking softly as if in a church, clutching the show's handout of information like a trail guide. The West of the photographs is the natural wonder there for the taking. The taking itself is seldom viewed as worth the talents of a photographer. We have raised up generations of them all blasting away at Yosemite or the Rockies or Death Valley or the silhouette of a saguaro. The focus is fine, the contrast perfect, the sharp teeth of our world almost always absent. No highways, no bulldozers, no beer cans, no men, no women, no children, no life. You can lean forward and stare into a thousand of these photographs and never once, not for a single second, catch the scent of a woman, the rot of a body, the raw fingers of an angry wind. Whenever I walk in the desert I think of the photographs because they seem magical—they express nothing that I see or feel or think as the hundreds of miles move through my body. They are the West of the mechanics. I am in the West of wetbacks, hot summer nights, the Border Patrol, the bats are squeaking over my head, and my feet hurt.

Finally, the man-catcher roars off and we are left to the silence of the land. It is absolute. Not a decibel of sound from an insect, not the faintest swish of the limbs of the creosote in the still air. The feet pound, our talk falls away, shooting stars blaze, and silence becomes a drug. The mind drifts. That is why we come, why we always come. The mind drifts.

We are in dreamland and once the Yumas, the big men with the big clubs, were the dreamers of this land. They felt the night thoughts were the fuel of their minds. One shaman explained it this way: "Before I was born I would sometimes steal out of my mother's womb while she was sleeping, but it was dark and I did not go far. Every good doctor begins to understand before he is born."

Fall into the dead world. As a boy he takes night trips to the mountain and sleeps at its base. He feels for his body with his two hands, but it is not there. Four days and four nights he moves up the mountain and comes upon the dark-house. Inside is the god, he peers into the blackness and can barely make out the form. The god is naked and huge and only the greatest shamans are with him—a crowd of lesser men stand outside. The boy continues to dream and in time he can go to the god at will. He lies down and soon he is up on the mountain with the crowd. The god tells him how the world began and other matters. He dreams the stories bit by bit and then he goes to the old men and tells them and they say, "That's right! I was there and heard it myself." If he is wrong, they say, "You dreamed badly. That is not right." And that is the way the gods teach the men and the land pours into the minds of the people.

I am walking, the miles float past, the bats sometimes squeak overhead, a freight rolls past, and then the silence, a black silence hugging the desert. The mind drifts. The Mexicans are moving around us, their abandoned water jugs are everywhere, but we do not see them. They pursue their own dreams of paychecks, new clothes, perhaps in a few months a trip back to the village with the cash. The women will beg them. The new immigration law has

swung into effect but there is no sense of it yet in the silence of the desert night. A Border Patrol truck races up,
spotlights blazing, and checks us out. The hunt. The driver
says they bagged one hundred fifty-three the night before
at a point up ahead. I speak and read Spanish poorly. I
believe in ketchup, I want the trains to run on time, and
yet for this night in this desert I am more kin to the Mexicans than the people of my own nation. I walk along lusting for my runaway and I wonder what went wrong. We
share the blackness, the silence, and the hunger, the grinding appetite in our gut that says there is always something
better ahead, always a reason to move on and taste new
ground.

Harris and his party are struggling, he has little time for
journal entries and they grow scant. An arm extends from
the sand, a bony thing severed from the body, and the
Texans gather round. The ligaments of the elbow are not
yet dry. The desert continues to pound their senses: their
path is lined with the mummified bodies of dead animals
that have been stood on their feet by comedians passing
through.

We snap alert briefly when a small sidewinder rattles in
our path. And then the silence returns. Around 3:00 A.M.
we go down. We are weary, the packs are heavy, the water
alone weighs twenty-odd pounds. And we are dry. We
drink water copiously but we cannot keep up. We fall
asleep on a flat field of stones.

At gray light, I slip from my bag and walk out into the
desert. I hear voices speaking Spanish in a nearby wash.
Two Mexicans emerge, and fade away to the north. Then
the sun comes on. A small Border Patrol plane buzzes us.
The hunt. The man stares down from his aluminum co-
coon. He is above the desert but he is not in it.

Miles from Glamis the sign begins, the ground torn,
crushed, hacked, and chewed by the peculiar fat-tired
tracks of all-terrain cycles. Fire marks appear where the

dune people have made their camps but the sites are empty. It is Monday morning, the Glorious Fourth is over, and the humans that gathered here for holidays have returned to their work. Paper plates are taped to the power-line poles with messages and arrows: SMITH, JONES, FUCK-HEAD, and so forth. The ground is more and more shredded by machines.

We reach Glamis at 9:30 A.M., bone weary. There is one store and the woman tending it says, "That dirt road by the tracks? Oh, you've come forty miles."

To the east loom the Chocolate Mountains (a military gunnery range), to the west the dunes. And in between Glamis, named after a Scottish castle, a dusty outpost of trailers, a few auto repair shops, and the store, the wonderful store full of beer and canned food and clothes. This is the heart of a culture, the Jerusalem of the dune people. They gather here at Thanksgiving in legendary numbers—the locals say 100,000, the skeptics figure 25,000—and they drink and roar about for days. For that holiday the store has eight cashiers working constantly. We are aliens here, men afoot in the nerve center of the desert machine world.

Inside, commingled with the food and camping supplies, are the totems of this desert culture: baseball caps. One features a pile of feces on the bill and the word SHIT-HEAD, another a cloth model of a vagina and the simple inscription INSPECTOR. There is a bleak replica of a penis and scrotum labeled DICKHEAD. Various T-shirts and shorts celebrate the sport—in dire need of a new garment I purchase a pair of women's shorts with large type announcing GLAMIS DUNE DOLL. The proprietor tosses in a T-shirt—I SURVIVED ANOTHER EXCITING WEEKEND IN GLA-MIS!

Her name is Catherine Theresa Le Blanc, she is fifty-six, has salt and pepper hair, and she loves to talk. She and her husband came here thirteen years ago and bought some dune for their own private duning. They would come out

at Christmas and roar about and hang Christmas ornaments on a creosote bush. We sit out front swatting flies
while she reviews her life. They began racing cars in 1952
and then drifted into the business of fixing race cars and
then re-engineering stock cars. They made a ton of
money—"I rich enough," she says, smiling, "I got a limou-
sine, I got blue ice diamonds." Arthritis reached into her
husband's hands and then when he'd be in the desert, the
condition would recede. They came to the desert.

He began to build huge sheet-metal buildings, and built
and built. There must be ten thousand square feet under
the roof now: their place, a daughter's place, the store, the
pizza parlor, and now he is toiling out back on the new
restaurant that will open in September. Cactus Katie—the
name given her, she explains, by one Navajo Joe—shows
us everything. The beer cooler big enough for Milwaukee,
the shop where her husband Beau works silently on his
current project, the chickens running about, and then the
garages, huge spaces, with the Cadillac, the Lincoln
stretch limo (vanity plates, Le Blanc on the floormat, the
wet bar and television), the fleet of dune machines, plus
two for working in rock, her son's collection of hot cars
and old trucks. Everything is covered with dust and seems
almost forgotten—objects seized and left aside like old
toys. The $40,000 dune buggy with the Porsche rear end
and twin turbos, it too is covered with dust. The alcohol-
burning Cobra, the Pantera, the Mustang named "Wild-
fire" with a custom paint job flaming off the side—all are
idle. I want to stay and caress the machines for hours.
Katie opens the door on the limo and I control the desire
to pitch camp in the back seat.

When they got married they had $24. They raced cars,
they worked, they made it. What they made here in the
desert has the feel of a temporary camp. The buildings, the
goods in the store, the bare ground scraped clean around
the business, all these things will be but a brief flicker of

the desert's life. It is a party, decorations everywhere, the guests arrive in T-shirts, halter tops, come roaring right up on homemade garage monsters lusting to conquer the sands. They dismount, amble in, drain a beer, talk loudly, celebrate. The desert waits. That is what it always does. A brief flicker. For me, of course, the spot will be an eyesore every day of my life and for decades thereafter. I will lament about how easy it is to scar the dry ground and how long the wounds persist. But this is human talk and has nothing to do with what takes place here. Katie has the blue ice diamonds, Beau has the $40,000 dune buggy, but the wind pouring off the sand with a furnace's breath, the desert, the godforsaken badlands, have the future and are all the God we are likely to meet.

And now Katie and Beau want to sell. They are asking $1.5 million down, $5 million total for the corner and the store. She has advertised in Japanese newspapers—"They have the money now, honey, they will buy anything."

We move to leave. She asks, "Where you headed?"

"To the dunes, we are going into the dunes."

"Where will you sleep?"

"In the dunes."

"You can't," she says fiercely, "the snakes are dangerous, and honey, the scorpions out there are the size of large shrimp. The heat will kill you."

A Mexican comes over from the railroad tracks, buys a can of food, and melts away again. She says, "They can do it. You can't."

We walk away into the late afternoon heat. The south side of the road is dunes and the dunes are nothing but tire tracks. Small trees huddle here and there like survivors of a blitzkrieg. On the north side of the highway, dune machines are banned by the Bureau of Land Management and the sand is carpeted with plants and every swell is anchored with shrubs. The lesson is very plain. But it is easy to deny. Cactus Katie insists that the machines promote plants, they stir up the soil and that is what makes things grow, you know?

We press higher into the sand and throw our bags down near the crest. Signs along the north side of the road ban machines. Some have been shot, some simply torn down. I admire the spunk of my countrymen. The wind keeps the particles glissading across the surface through the night and the moon bounces off the soft forms.

To the west the lights of the Imperial Valley bloom in the night sky. I look east. I run through a short rosary of reasons to be on this sand in this summer night: there are the hospital bills that must be paid; expenses that must be confronted. These are reasons. But the motive is something else. I must get out, I must walk out of my office and fling myself into something I cannot predict and cannot control and cannot stop. I am curled deep in a bowl of sand, nestled and safe from everyone and everything. I think: They cannot reach me here. I have no idea who "they" might be. The noise has stopped, the letters, conversations, phone calls that all reinforce what everyone insists is already true. Here there is possibility because no one cares what it means or even that it exists. Here I am safe from the boredom of belonging.

I always want to go to the dunes for the same reasons other people avoid them. They have no fixed form, they shift under your feet, and if you lie down the little grains of sand slowly toss past in the wind and bury you. You become lost in the swells, cannot tell your direction after a while, lose any sure sense of advance. There is no shade. Nothing beckons, every direction promises more of the same. I sleep deeply in the dunes. Always. Here I am safe.

Early the next morning, we leave the dunes behind and enter the creosote flats that the Navy uses for a bombing range. Big signs announce that the area is salted with live bombs and dangerous for people to blunder around in.

Here the tracks of the dune machines finally stop. And then the bombing range ends and the Imperial Valley rolls before us green and empty.

We are weary of the heat, it is high noon. But we push on. Harris cannot take any more and camps on the desert. A party of Sonorans comes up on the Texans and they electrify the men with assurances that much gold abounds in the Sierra. One mule sags under the weight of his packs and the packs hold nothing but gold nuggets.

After a while I notice there are no hawks. I am lying on the ground under the shade of a tamarisk and I look up and realize I have seen no hunters in the sky. There is nothing for them to eat. The fields of the Imperial Valley are green, the flies are a plague (retiring only at night to turn the late shift over to the mosquitoes), and the earth is in many ways sterile. No rats, no mice, no prey.

We walk through the 114-degree heat and stop at a small store. The sign says closed and inside I see the owner sitting at the bar sipping a beer and staring off into space. We throw down our packs, lie in the shade, and he swiftly appears. He says this is a business, not a public park. The eyes are small and full of disappointments. A thermometer over the door stalls at 112 degrees. We buy some pop and he mellows slightly. He is closed all summer long—he bought the place two years before. Why do you close in the summer?

"Because," he snaps, "there are twenty fucking people in eight fucking square miles."

The emptiness.

For miles and miles we see no one. The fields are perfect, the houses tidy and sheltered by trees, the earth all but silent. Finally, we hit a sign of life—new ranchstyle home, wrought-iron fence, two fierce German shepherds patrolling the yard—next to a big lot full of machines. A man works on a tractor. Can we sit in the shade of your tree?

"For how long," he demands.

"Fifteen minutes?"

He nods.

A few miles more and we come upon a rundown house. Three Mexican men work on a car, the lot is full of wounded vehicles. We walk up and ask for water, pointing to the faucet in the yard. No one speaks English. A man walks up, says nothing, takes my bottle and disappears. He returns with a jug of ice water.

The sun fries my brain, I stumble along, the fields are empty, achingly empty. A store looms off to the side, and we stagger over. Our feet hurt, our minds skitter, and we crave fluid. We enter. The bar is lined with tattooed men wearing denim vests, big knives strapped to their legs, pistols stuffed in their pockets, and wallets secured by chains with the girth of logging cables. I look down at my shorts shouting GLAMIS DUNE DOLL, consider my cap which displays a .45 crossed with a .38 and the words REDNECKS FOR SOCIAL RESPONSIBILITY.

I decide I am dead.

A woman shoves out the long necks; her T-shirt queries: GOOD GIRL? BAD GIRL! She is very skinny, the hips lean, breasts small, the face rough with life, and sour eyes tell everyone her smile is a lie. Her kid, around four or five, raises hell on the floor, and in between opening beers she gives the boy a steady stream of corrections. It seems he has done nothing right and never will. She eyes me like a piece of meat and I can tell by her expression that I am not prime or choice.

A huge guy weighing in around three hundred pounds leans toward her and wonders if she'd like to party tonight. On his arm is a large tattoo advocating INDIAN POWER. His name is Brew, he wears a ponytail, has the regulation pig sticker lashed to his leg and a .38 Special stuffed in his back pocket. He is from a reservation near San Diego and is a Diegueño. How do you spell that, sir?

Fuck, I don't know. I do not ask him his dreams.

The back bar hosts jars of long-deceased eggs and sausages ground from hogs during the presidency of Millard Fillmore. Brew hails from heroic stock: his ancestors attacked the mission at San Diego within a month of its founding and were noted by the despairing priests as proud, boastful, given to quarrels, and hard to handle. Brew is a little weak on the tribe's history but he noticeably brightens when I mention the '49ers who sometimes croaked in these hostile sands. He came to the Valley three years ago to kind of hide out for a few months. He drives a tow truck and his eyes are filmed over from an afternoon of dedicated drinking. His T-shirt celebrates the Grateful Dead.

The leader of the pack is simply Larry, who explains there is nothing out on him except maybe a warrant for cat torture. He is forty something, clad in Levis, T-shirt, cap, the face a beard, a fat gut slopping over his belt and a fifteen-inch bowie knife on his hip. He frowns at my beverage, a jug of Gatorade. The Snickers bar chaser does not help my standing.

His son sidles up to discuss a blown head gasket and Larry proudly announces that the boy was twenty years old before he concluded he had raised the baby and not the afterbirth. We go back into the empty fields. About a mile down the pike, Larry roars past with a young girl on his bike. His face is a stern mask, the eyes blacked out by sunglasses, and he does not wave. He is doing Marlon Brando in *The Wild One*.

I awaken sometime the next day in a motel in Brawley. The town was laid out in 1902 by the Imperial Land Company. They'd bought the ground from an L.A. banker, J.H. Brayley, and proudly told him they were going to name the community after him. He strenuously objected. So they made the Y a W and the result is Brawley. About twenty thousand people call the place home and Main

Street is a monument to the late twenties and early thirties.

The voices on Main Street say the town is stagnant and needs some light industry, that the big growers all live in nice houses in the southwest corner of Brawley and don't give a damn about it growing and control everything and keep the place stale. And there is nobody out on the land, just machines and hay, and that means there is nobody to come into town and buy things. The east side of town, just across the tracks, is the Mexican end.

"Mexicans?" one woman offers. "They do everything, they'll sweep, they'll clean. If you got a job, the word gets out."

The problems are kind of simple. Salt in the irrigation water stays behind in the ground, builds up, and keeps killing the fields. Then you've got to dig trenches and put in tubes of tiles under the fields to drain off the salts and this slop flows into the Salton Sea which keeps getting more polluted and New River just west of town has just been called the dirtiest river in the world by "Sixty Minutes." One woman chuckles, "You sit by New River a while and you can see just about anything float by." As a bonus, Mexicali, just across the border, pours its sewage into the stream. A farmer weighs in, your basic Imperial Valley man—he tills 19,000 acres—and he sketches the season to date: "The beet people made money, early melon people made money, hay people held steady, and Sudan grass people went to hell in a hand basket."

I attend to my trousseau—I have walked right through my socks—and enter Ellis's: Ready to Wear for the Entire Family, Since 1915. Mitchell Ellis is sixty-two, has skin like fine paper and a soft, sad voice. He has been running the family business since 1948.

He says, "I didn't want to, I had ideas and they would have worked. If you can make it here, you can make it anywhere. I was going to USC and there were people, lei-

sure time and people. I had these ideas—wholesale
schemes, various investment plans for property—but I
had to come back and take over the family business. I've
always advised others, young people, to go elsewhere, and
each person who has followed my advice has done excellent."

Ellis mentions the town's dark legend, Dr. Ben L. Yellen,
M.D. Around the corner is his office—Physician, Surgeon/
Medico, Cirijuano. He is in his late seventies now but fifteen years ago he was elected to the city council and put
forth a simple idea: enforce the 160-acre federal law lim-
iting the size of farms in government-created irrigation
districts. He said the big holdings were choking the town
to death and that small farms would produce people and
people would mean business for Main Street. At meetings,
he was hooted down and some locals think it is a wonder
he wasn't killed. Now he is a ghost in the town. The medi-
cal office is closed—he was recently stripped of his license
and is fighting for its return—and no one is sure where he
can be found.

I chase him like a ghost around town. The library offers
up folders of yellowed clippings. A barber tells me he may
be at the senior citizens' center. I walk into a bar, the sign
neon, the interior a monument to drunks of the 1930s. A
shuffleboard table lines one wall and dedicated boozers,
all Anglos, drain their whiskey in a bath of country music.
The good doctor's office is across the street but where is
he? No one knows and who cares. The woman tending bar
smiles a lot and that helps. I can taste the past in here and
yet sense the place has no history. That is why Ben Yellen
is forgotten; he tried to rise up in Brawley and join history.
And this is not the place for such activity. That is a fact of
the West, the place said to have a rich history, one which
nobody cares to remember.

Of course, Ben Yellen lost his fight, just as the farmers
will lose theirs to the relentless desert and the salts that

slowly strangle the field. At this end of the Imperial Valley the land is going increasingly into hay and after that there is maybe barley and then you run out of crops that can stand the salt in the soil. There is an air of death on this landscape, and each trickle of the Colorado River brings the end nearer.

The Valley has 458,386 acres drinking off the flow of the river and throws off a song of American appetites. This is the place for beans, black-eyed peas, broccoli, cabbage, carrots, cauliflower, celery, collards, cucumbers, corn, eggplant, endive, fava beans, fennel, garlic, herbs, lettuce, melons, mustard, okra, onions, parsley, parsnips, peas, peppers, radishes, rutabagas, sesame, spinach, squash, sweet basil, Swiss chard, thyme, tomatoes, turnips, and waterlilies. Come here for artichokes, asparagus, grapefruit, lemons, oranges, tangerines, dates, grapes, guar beans, jojoba, palms, peaches, pecans, for alfalfa, barley, bermuda grass, clover, cotton, rape, rye, sorghum, soybeans, Sudan grass, sugar beets, and wheat.

Benjamin Harris and his party move through Brawley and see desert. They are starving to death and about to die of thirst. The parched corn sticks in their throats and the beasts look at them with envy as they devour the feed. They cannot see the town, none of what I see exists yet, they cannot hear the trickling of the water in the ditches, eye the endless fields of straight rows.

The Imperial Valley holds the ultimate American terror—complete victory in all its attendant emptiness. The dreamers are gone.

Brawley is split by the tracks and east of the railroad is Mexican town. The first block is a row of rough bars renowned in the Valley for homicide, drugs, and general high spirits. This is the holding pen for people whose jobs have been devoured by machines. The Monte Carlo Café is dark, men drink quietly at the bar, an old woman sells menudo, the soup—made from the lining of a cow's stomach, hominy, and a couple of hooves—that is the traditional cure for a hangover. The bartender hops about in short shorts and a halter. In back there are two tables, one full of Mexicans playing cards, one dominated by old Filipino men. The men at the bar are young, their faces black with stubble, the bones sharp, the eyes hunting. Their papers do not bear inspection. Perhaps they have a green card making work legal, perhaps they do not. It is hours till sundown and they are drinking, that slow, patient drinking that is meant to build steadily toward poetry and song and a fist and a knife. The kind of drinking that reveals a caring person. If you stay, and are quiet but friendly, and then you probe ever so politely, each blank face will have a story. There will be a town or village, a place name with a caravan of letters arranged in a half Spanish–half Indian row, a spot you have not heard of. They will speak very affectionately of this place where they were born. If you produce a map, they will never be able to find their birthplace, they do not know the world of maps. They know the ground. Then, this courtesy of origins out of the way, they will tell you why they left, and the talk will have a laughing kind of lilt but the words will have an anger. This will be plain in their dark eyes. They are the hungry ones, the ones who refused, who did not listen to the caution of the women. They are the men who left. They never will have heard of Nacho—he is not of their village—but they will have a part of his face in their face. Just outside the saloon door there is that party of Sonorans riding past, the saddlebags filled with gold. The men in the bar do not know this fact, but if told, they would feel no surprise.

Brawley is a leaden cloak that hangs off the shoulders of the residents. I slowly grasp the fact: a century of American energy, hundreds of millions of dollars, giant canals, big dams, and the busy federal bureaucrats have created a zone of boredom, hay fields, unemployment, and resignation.

The sun is slowly starting to set as Anna goes to work.
She is twenty-three and leans against a car fender slurping a huge Pepsi. A pickup rolls up, she pours into the open window, there are quick words but no agreement, the truck speeds away. On her wrist is a six-inch scar—"I got in a gang fight when I was fourteen. I won. The operation cost six thousand dollars." She is heavy from her recent pregnancy, a girl born in February, and her arms and face are studded with tattoos: blue dots on her chin, both wrists, and on one shoulder the name Juana for her mother and her child. The other says BROLE, the name local Hispanics use for Brawley. She says she kicked heroin and cocaine a few month back. I do not believe her. The words tumble out quickly and in a flat tone as if she were racing through her morning rosary.

She comes from a family of nine kids, her dad drives a tractor, an uncle is a bartender across the street. The face radiates intelligence and ruin and I am drawn to her. Flesh hangs off her soft frame but the eyes cut like a knife. We do not speak of the business. Her words are very tired. I want to know what she has learned but I never will. The price of such knowledge is all over her body.

I am drawn to her. We talk, a car pulls up with two blond-haired Anglo kids, the radio blaring. They beckon, she ambles over, leans in to discuss possible business, then straightens up and walks back. They laugh and race away. She says nothing of her brief errand. The child interests me. I have a son, two months old now as I stand with Anna in the 110-degree Brawley street as dusk seeps across the town. I have not kicked my heroin or cocaine—I am here, not bouncing a baby on my knee. When I walk in the desert night I see his round face, feel the efforts of his dark eyes to focus. But I do not break stride. I sense what it is like to bring a child into a life where you are incapable of making the right amount of room.

"The cops?" her flat, yet soft, voice asks. "They don't bother much, they're all rookies now and scared of the people. I'm just going to stay here and raise the kid in this heat. I left in '79 for the Job Corps, that's where I got these tattoos—I wish I could get rid of them—and I spent the time in San Diego. I came back here."

San Diego: the name spins my mind. I am strolling down the city's Fourth Avenue, the neon sign says Golden West Hotel. I look into the lobby, a long, bare strip of small white tiles leading up to the forbidding desk which is festooned with big signs warning guests of all the devilish things they must not do in their rooms. Two women about thirty sit on a hard wood bench, their legs crossed. They look up into my eyes and consider if I mean business. San Diego has always been where Americans go to escape America and find they have run out of country. It is a trap where you can sit in the sun or play racquet ball or raise flowers. You can do anything you want except matter. One year was enough for Anna.

"I like working outdoors more than indoors," she continues. "I don't really have any problems, I just take my days as they come. Get cut up? Naw, I'm from around here. The block? I'd rather have them knock it down. It's not right for kids growing up to see what happens around here. I don't want my kid to go through what I've gone through. I don't know what I want to do. I don't want you to tell people what I really do. Tell them I make two hundred forty dollars a month on welfare. How much is that an hour? You figure it out. You can divide."

It is dawn at New River and the sign says: WATER POLLUTED, DO NOT ENTER. Benjamin Harris feels differently. He is half dead and standing on the bank: "We found a river running from the left to right. . . . It was New River, which we had been told had not run for ninety years. The Mexicans said the miracle was especially designed for American emigrants on whose side Providence had arrayed itself. . . ."

We stagger forward into Providence. Seven miles of flies

brings us to Westmorland, a town of about a thousand souls on the edge of the Imperial Valley. This is hay country. I sit in the café listening to farmer talk. We are objects of curiosity—You walked out in that heat? From Yuma? Jesus Christ, you crazy boy? We are hired on as the village idiots and thus held harmless enough for conversation.

The woman has large, square, rimless glasses, is in her forties, and moved here in May from Austin, Texas. "It's been a disaster," she confides. "My moron husband had this idea. He's been a trucker for years and the money was good but he was always gone and that wasn't so good. So he got this big idea for hauling hay and he worked at his drawing table and designed this truck that does everything—load, unload, what-have-you—and then he went and sunk a ton of money in building such a truck. So we came to Westmorland—God, just once I'd like to move to a place like Vermont, you know, I've never been there but I've seen pictures of the trees and green and little villages—but we came here because they raise a lot of hay. But nobody here was interested because they're all renegades around here and do things their own way. Then he found another hay area and they liked the new truck but it didn't matter because the haying was over there, so there was nothing to haul. Now he's doing charcoals of World War II fighter planes and a friend of his says he'll fly them around the country and help sell them. Which is fine because I can sell furniture and clothes and lots of things but I can't sell art. I don't know art, I don't understand artists. I appreciate art, sure, but I don't know how to sell it."

So they are in a dead stall. All the money is tied up in the truck and no one wants the machine, and so she sits there for hours, smoking cigarettes, drinking coffee, and composing a letter to the folks back home.

I wander down to Back Street, the old whoring district of the town. Forty years ago, when the fields were garden crops instead of hay, the town was surrounded by Filipino work camps and on the weekend the men came in and wanted women. "Those Filipinos," one local chuckles, "they were a gold mine. They'd come in about thirty seconds." A merchant in Brawley made a tidy sum selling the women cases of slippers with little pom-poms on the toes so they could walk up and down the street. An earthquake in April 1978 (6.3 on the Richter scale) toppled all but two of the old brothels.

John Martin, eighty-one, and his wife Edith, eighty, remember those days well. "The girls," the old man explains, "would come up once a month and pay the cops fifty or a hundred bucks—it was listed as a fine. Pretty near every shack on Back Street had a girl in it. In that day and time, the Filipinos did all the work here—they all drove good automobiles, 'course it took ten of them to pay for it and on a Saturday evening you couldn't find a parking place. There were maybe five hundred people here then but if you took a census on a Saturday evening, it would be a son-of-a-bitch.

"The Filipinos would line up, say fifteen or twenty of them, and the head Filipino would ask, 'How much for all my men?' The girls charged a dollar. It started around '32 or '35. They were all white girls, good-looking girls."

We are sitting out back on the porch. It's about 110 and Edith walks down to garden and comes back with fresh grapes from her arbor. She helped out at the houses. "I remember one madam, Carol, real well. She wore a shift, nothing but a shift, and owned land around UCLA. She typed scripts too for Hollywood. My, she loved her cats and birds. I helped in the tailor shop and we bought bolts of satin, the Filipinos loved the feel of satin. The girls had new dresses a couple of times a week. We cut out maybe ten or fifteen dresses a day. The girls had to stay on Back Street but they could come down to the beauty salon one day a week."

She cannot stop now. The past stands there with us in

the boiling air, a bony hand extends and caresses our faces, the air is rich, perfumed.

"I saw one madam bring in two girls from Louisiana— neither was more than sixteen—and they had hair down to their hips and the Filipinos loved to get their hands in that hair. I remember Shirley. She was murdered down at the White Wing Court. She drove a huge car and she kept her boy in a private school in L.A. She was yellow—it's funny, her mother was black as tar, and her boy was black as tar, but she was yellow. Shirley was beat to death. Nobody ever investigated. It looked like she'd been beat with fists.

"The Filipinos are gone now. And so are the whores. But it was something back then. Every year the Filipinos got out on the bridge at the edge of town and stopped traffic for the March of Dimes—one year they raised two thousand dollars. They'd turn it all over.

"Nobody ever raided their cock fights."

The summer heat flows over the town, a pudding of lava. The grapes burst in my mouth with sweetness and the two old people talk on about the time when Westmorland was men lined up with hot loins on Saturday night.

Back Street is boarded up. The White Wing Court is now a tumble-down motel packed with old cars that haven't been washed in a few years. The main street rumbles with semis hauling loads of hay from town. Outside the café sits the hay truck designed by the man from Texas, the truck no one wants.

The sun starts to lose some of its fire and we walk out of town. To the west we see the desert and mountains beyond. Mosquitoes devour us and we yearn for the desert. Ben Harris and his men are full of water and hope but the desert does not cheer them. "We got a direct view of the mountain foothills," he jots down, "wearing an appearance more sorrowful than I ever dreamed nature could express."

We walk fast, stomping our way out of the Valley. No hawks, not a single hawk. At 9:00 P.M. the fields end and we throw down our bags on raw earth and listen to the whisper of the creosote.

A sheet of flame rises off my ankle. The tendon is going. The desert has been kind: I am being butchered by the highway, a victim of the slant of the pavement. By the time I realize what is happening, it is too late, I cannot contain the damage. I begin to limp. The heat is, we move through it, we drink water, we belong. The flies are gone, they've stayed home in the Imperial Valley along with the mosquitoes. Off to the right, the Salton Sea sits like glass, and around us there is creosote, an ocean of greasewood.

We are entering Cahuilla country, an umbrella name for the various bands that used the mountains to the west, used the palm groves huddled in the canyons, and during moments when water seeped into the sink, used the Salton basin. The sun is a white force. The mind glazes over and tumbles through new contortions. Everything starts with darkness, a sweet darkness, and then a wonderful singing comes forth from the blackness. The darkness divides into two forms, male and female, and then come the colors, red, white, blue, brown. Language fills the air, Cahuilla, the original tongue of all human beings. That is how it begins for the Cahuilla people.

They are dreamers, too. The young men in the rite of passage taste of the Jimson weed—datura—and bring back visions. Sometimes the dose is too high and young men die. It seems that once no one in the Southwest had much time for anything but dreams. Harris is feeling better now. He and his friends have fled the desert for the foothills to the west. They find an old man and then the old man gives a command and the Indian women dance, the bare feet pounding the ground in unison. They chant and the Texans find the whole thing ridiculous. The feet continue to pound.

We stay in the desert. There is no reason beyond appetite. Things have not yet happened here, the ground is greasewood, the land a plastic form of soil. And the heat is necessary. The Highway Patrol roars up from time to time, chastising us for being afoot in the desert—"You can't walk, it's against the law"—and then drives off. The tendon screams, I drag the leg. Around noon we hit a hut. The Border Patrol is at work: a checkpoint, America's shot at a Berlin Wall.

The agents are friendly, we crack jokes, they consider putting us in their jail so we can be cool but then change their minds—federal regulations, you know.

We sit in the shade. A Greyhound bus arrives, all red, white, and blue. I look through the window and see two men with quick, nervous eyes. They pull them off, they are about forty, one wearing a T-shirt that says, HAULIN' ASS. They go in the cage.

The feds average about one person per busload. The losers accept defeat. For them it is a very early in the game and they will be back, again and again.

We walk off into the 1:00 P.M. heat. This is the prime time, the land goes flat, the light crushes everything, the asphalt boils up through our shoes. The Salton Sea just sits there, a cauldron of all the poisons we can dump on the land of the Imperial Valley. It is a fiasco, a sea where the fish are thought by some agencies to be too toxic for human consumption—America's Dead Sea, but one lacking the legend of a Christ.

Salton City arrives at dusk. We are empty, drink four beers in a few minutes and sleep on a vacant lot. There are many. Twenty-seven years ago Salton City was launched and it is still waiting to leave the dock. It is the basic Sunbelt real estate dream, a dull grid of vacant lots owned by absentee owners, each waiting for the other guy to build the first house. In the winter a couple of thousand snowbirds drag their campers here and squat. In the summer, the sun takes the land back.

The last time I am here it is the early sixties, I have fled the house, am sixteen or seventeen, and we lie drunk on the beach by the Sea. We are hauling an old man to Los Angeles. He is a juicer, a dishwasher fed up with the backroom toil of a Tucson café. He has this dream. He has read that Los Angeles is plagued by smog and in his beat-up suitcase he has the answer—the plans for a steam car. His face is stubble, his hair gray, his nose the artwork of a dedicated rummy. We sit on the sand amid a heap of beer cans. He will solve the problem, it is all in his suitcase. Dreams.

The heat takes us down. Cars whiz past blind to our presence. We are the danger, the man by the road who will kill the driver, then rape the women, carve messages in the soft flesh with the blade of a dirty knife. There is no shade, the sun flows in waves across the ground. I clamber down into a wash, crawl into a small culvert, and curl up in the cool darkness. The stove lights, a hot cup of coffee pours down my throat. Flames explode at the end of the tube where the desert incinerates in the afternoon. I could live here forever.

Ten miles brings us to Desert Shores, another retirement haven waiting for the future to arrive. The tendon now sizzles for about fourteen inches along my leg. I drag the foot. I am finished and I know it, a road kill of the American highway. The café is pleasant, cool, and I drink ice tea by the barrel.

At first the man does not speak and then we stumble into a conversation. He is a big man, perhaps six foot, five inches and solid, and wears his fifty-some years with a certain zest. He came out of West Virginia and served twenty-two years in the Navy. Three tours ('67, '68, '72) as a field adviser to South Vietnamese troops took its toll.

"If you think the Vietnamese don't value life," he says, "try and kill one."

My leg is screaming.

I disappear into the rice paddies of Nam. The man is in that mood, the one where he is not talking to me, he is just talking, and my job is to be the perfect stranger that will hear his tale and then vanish from his life, the person he can speak to about his dark thoughts and yet never have to face again. His wife is sitting next to him and the expression on her face says simply, I have never heard this before. Her eyes at first grow large and then begin to shrink. I think she would like to shut them.

He arrived in Vietnam in the morning, was sent out on patrol that day with troops from the South Vietnamese Army, and did not come back for one hundred six days. That first year he spent two hundred seventy-seven days in the paddies and jungle, plus thirty-three more in the hospital for wounds.

"I remember one time I was wounded in '67 and the doc said, 'Well, I can get my knife and needle and thread and fix the wound, that's easy, it's right out of the book. But I can't fix you that easily.' And I knew what he meant."

He would be the only round-eye about and for weeks his life was the villages. His men did not understand the war or democracy or South Vietnam. They understood the village. They would ask him, "What is Saigon?" His first tour ends in Saigon and he is to leave in the morning. Tet begins, he is in the streets, for seven days and nights the war comes to town and he cannot get out. He fears his number is about up, he can feel death touching his shoulder. He has been here too long. His buddies commandeer a jeep, they roar out to the airport brandishing their weapons. He climbs aboard a cargo plane. He is alone—the rest of the passengers are in body bags. He weighs one hundred sixty pounds.

Fisherman keep coming into the café, their caps announcing they'd rather be out on the sea. They drink coffee and smoke and the Navy man from Vietnam keeps talking. He does not fish. He lives by the Sea now and he watches. He is retired. And he watches. The fires have not all banked. He hates the Border Patrol, their roadblocks gnaw at him. He fought a war so that he could come home and be stopped by goddamn roadblocks? The Border Patrol are a bunch of amateurs walking around with loaded guns. He remembers a time in Yuma back in 1976.

"I was there for one of those businessman seminars—I was out of the service and setting myself up. And we broke for a snack that evening before we went into our night session. I walked up the stairs and turned down the hallway toward my room and there was one of those Border Patrol guys—you know they have like these SWAT teams—this guy standing there all dressed up in camouflage and face paint and an M-16 in his hands and something snapped in me, you know, and I grabbed that carbine and slammed it against his throat—he later told me he figured he was dead—and I jerked it back and was fixing to bayonet him—it didn't have one, but it did in my head—when the two guys with him yelled something and that brought me out of it. The two guys with him were outfitted too and had M-16s, but they hadn't even reacted to what I was fixing to do. I told them, I said, you silly sons-of-bitches, you got no right to go around this way if you can't even react."

He talks evenly and only when he gets to the incident at Yuma does the voice rise and fall. He is finished now, he has said what he needs to say. And he goes, leaving me in the Colorado desert with the mist off the rice paddies hanging around me. I am suffocating.

I look west out the window at the nearby mountains. Once there were grizzly bears up there and the Cahuilla called the bears "great, great-grandfather." When they came upon one, they would speak softly and urge the bear to retreat further into the mountains and hide so that no harm could come to it. Harris is somewhere off in there now, in the early morning light he sights a gray mass in a tree. He raises the rifle, fires, and out topples a bird with a nine-foot wing span. Benjamin Harris has slaughtered a California Condor.

A few hundred yards to the north, the vineyards of the Coachella Valley begin. The desert is over now. There is sun but soon there will be orderly rows and the stench of chemicals. Everything is organized. A few miles back in the desert there was a billboard. It said: DEVELOPMENT NEEDED.

The strip towns now come on—Indio, La Quinta, Palm Desert, Rancho Mirage, Cathedral City, Palm Springs. My ankle has swollen to generous proportions. I hitch. I look out the truck window and see the final dreamland of my nation, the place where presidents come like ancient elephants to die amidst used-up comedians, actors, and singers. This is the celebrated spot, the one with the color ads beckoning the rich and bored to come and play in the sun, to leave that martini on the counter of the New York bar, leave it right now and jet out here to do a hot tub with a blonde, always a blonde. The strip cities probably have more blondes having less fun than any place outside of Sweden.

Bob Hope's huge ugly house—kind of like the world's fattest butterfly—stares down from a ridge, Sinatra has a street named after him. This is the trophy case for my America. I talk to a hack, nine years driving limos for the stars, and he drifts off into a tirade about Jack Lemmon, a slob, a drunk, a piece of meat. Now Wayne, the Duke, he was class, and the guy grows misty-eyed at being the driver for the last bout of true grit, Wayne's eulogy for American hungers, *The Shootist.* My ears grow large, I teethed on John Wayne movies.

I am sitting at a table by the pool of the Spa Resort in Palm Springs. This is Agua Caliente country, a Cahuilla band that once used the hot springs for voyages deep into their minds. Now the band has divided their land, leased it, some to become very rich, some to lose everything, and the hotel encases the tribal waters in cement, marble, and stone. People sun by the pool like racks of drying fish and there are no Indians in sight. There is Bob. He is thirty-three, bearded, and a tech for Motorola down here to computerize the sprinkler system at a local golf course. We drink Coronas and Bob talks. He is the Age of Aquarius marching along smartly in the Age of Wall Street. I have come out of the desert starved for dreams. And now I meet a dreamer and find this stuff is different in the eighties. It has moved from the loins to the place that knows no flesh. I try to be philosophic about this fact, but I am not good at philosophy. I dislike Bob on sight. He is not hungry, he has never been hungry. That is what I think. He has been . . . pinched, afraid, cautious, closed. His eyes, there are no backrooms in his eyes. Now Nacho, in his eyes there is no warmth, not a flicker. But there looms a maze of backrooms.

"I go to the meeting of the Rainbow people every year, every Fourth of July, and each year it's in a different state and every year at the end of the meeting everyone gets in a circle together and picks the next state and place, and you have to hitch, you have to suffer when you go, you have to purge yourself to get in the right place, and when you're in the right space, then you get there. Like one year I hitched across the United States and in Wyoming I got in a truck with a drunk in this raging rainstorm and two or three times I wanted to get out, I thought I was going to get killed, but I didn't and then I just couldn't stand it anymore and I got out and walked into this café and there were two girls there and they were going to the Rainbow meeting too, and until then I didn't even know where it was being held. Like I said, you gotta purge yourself and get in the right space."

The lime in my beer is a yearning green. I look up and

see a woman with large breasts in a yellow bikini. She rubs her brown flesh with suntan lotion, the fingers lazily caressing her skin. Her eyes drift over and briefly lock. Bob keeps talking. I drain a beer. The brown of her skin looks rich against the bright yellow fabric. The beers pull me safely into the night. I walk outside the hotel, Palm Springs is dead until fall. The stores are shut, the bars closed by 9:00 P.M. and on the main drag, kids sit on car hoods waiting for their lives to begin. I find an expensive restaurant, the waiter reads the French menu with a Spanish accent. I spill the wine and red fingers of Cabernet race across the tablecloth.

It is 5:00 A.M. and I wait by the mineral spring. The walls are gray, the spring a blue eye surrounded by chaise lounges, the water 106 degrees. Harris has crossed into the Central Valley, eaten elk, gotten wolfish from his meat diet, and is zeroing in on the gold fields. He will arrive there in September. The moon hangs over the San Jacinto Mountains. Long ago a woman came to the Cahuilla and taught them many things and was beloved and then she left and became the moon because the woman was a goddess. That is all past now, of course. The Cahuilla are local landlords, have lost the language, and across the street is the Patencio Office Building, named after one of their last great singers who took the old songs to his grave with him.

The drift of things became obvious a long time ago. Juan Manuel was a great Cahuilla leader and he threw his lot in with the Americans. In February 1863, he died of small-pox in the nearby pass where the Interstate now pours the traffic of the continent into the L.A. basin. No one buried him. Pigs and dogs ate his corpse.

He is not remembered.

I eye the blue water. The Cahuilla had this notion about the moon in a certain phase when it lingered at daybreak and could be seen upon the water, that at such moments if you dove for the reflection it would be good luck. I am poised. Beyond the spa wall, the rumble of garbage trucks floods the air, punctuated now and then by beeping as they back up. I can see the moon framed by two palm trees on the surface of the pool. I dive, the water is fat with minerals and tastes harsh in my mouth. I surface with the moon across my face. I look up at the goddess. Harris is full of bounce now, he jots in his journal, "If you ain't bold, you git no gold." The harbor at San Francisco is clogged with abandoned sailing ships, the crews having fled to the dreams of the Sierra. The last hard act of American history is about to unfold: when we run out of country, bump up against the Pacific, and have to face the rough fact of living with ourselves and with this ground. A Mexican in rubber boots is hosing down the spa area. The light comes on and the moon begins to fade from the pool.

Soon it will be our dreamless age again in Palm Springs. The land will be carpeted with condos, townhouses, pleasure palaces, and golf courses. the past will sink down into the sand and lie there mute and scorned. We have walked maybe one hundred twenty or one hundred thirty miles, hitched another thirty or forty. My wet suit clings to me, GLAMIS DUNE DOLL sparkles in big white letters, the hotel begins to revive for another day of sun and booze at poolside. The '49ers will retreat into lore, a motif for urban saloons, a catch phrase for American adventure. And we will be left with dune buggies, poisoned fields, hay trucks no one wants, towns gone flat and left behind by history. No one will dream, absolutely no one. It has been a long time since a fetus slipped away from the womb and went walking on the mountain, generations since the young boys drank datura and risked their lives to see through the rock and soil and heat into the dream.

We are very tired. But this is not the problem. It is the dreams. We must dream.

Before I left Brawley I could not sleep, the town weighed on me like an ancient grief, and I left my motel

and wandered the empty streets. I came upon a dark build- ing. Loud music skipped across the hard floor and in back
I found a bar and disco. The crowd was young, white, and
Valley, the spawn of rich growers. I was dirty, my T-shirt a
canvas of various naps on the ground, my hair a kind of
wire encased in soil. My eyes were bloodshot. I sat at the
bar and began to drink, drink very fast, one belt after another. I was desperate for the drunk. I thought of Anna a
few blocks away working the night at curbside. On the
wall was a portrait of John Wayne, the Duke, and I stared
into his face, a place of dreams for Americans. The bartender was a woman and she served me like a leper. This
did not matter. If I stared at John Wayne, I could imagine
the world before Brawley, the place of can-do, of futures,
new diggings, new farms, new lusts, the America that was
becoming, not the America that was a finished thing.

I remember *The Shootist.* He is very old, an ancient gun-
fighter, and cancer eats at his guts. A boy marvels that
Wayne is only an average shot and wonders how he got his
reputation as a killer.

"I was willing," the Duke explains.

I drink my booze. Willing. I put my head on the bar and
dream. The staff throws me out.

We have quit listening to the dreams. I flee the spa, the
hotel staff is marshalling to kill the day with towels, cold
drinks, piped-in music, various lotions for the flesh. I must
run. Harris and his Texans are only a few days ahead. I
can catch up. The moon is still on my face.

I am willing.

> *I'm a walking in the rain,*
> *Tears are falling and I feel the pain,*
> *Wishing you were here by me*
> *To end this misery.*
> *And I wonder*
> *I Wa-Wa-Wa-Wa-Wonder*

Why Wha-Wha-Wha-Wha Why
She ran away.
And I wonder, where she will stay,
My little runaway
Run, run, run, run, runaway.
          —"Runaway," Del Shannon

NACHO

Lupita lives in a small house in Tucson with a new Corvette outside. She sells drugs, tends bar, gets by. When Art first visits, her son lounges on the couch watching morning cartoon shows with a .38 stuffed in his jeans. Art is temporarily unnerved, his eyes chart the simple tract house like it is a maze, picking out escape routes, things to duck behind. He is here to talk to the mother, and the son, so careless and relaxed with that idle pistol, the son is something he had not counted on. Art does not have his piece, he is naked. He begins to feel tense, and then, he feels alive.

She is about forty and favors tight jeans, and running shoes. Her lavender T-shirt has a naked woman stretched out on hot sands and the words SUN YOUR BUNS. Her hair is blond, the eyes wary. The voice is soft, uncertain at times in English, but even in Spanish barely audible. We are in a café, the waitresses hustle about throwing silver and plates down.

She has difficulty recalling the past because it has ceased to exist. It is a finished thing. Nacho? Oh, yes, I've known since he was a boy, since he was nine years old. She would go down to Colonia Buenos Aires and visit the family. And later, when Nacho was a grown man, he would stay with her in Tucson for long stretches of time. They shared the similar interests, dealing drugs. She herself is Tucson-born but Nogales is like an extension of her house, a room on the south wing of her life.

The woman is careful in her words and puzzled. Why do we ask? Life has been hard. Her father raped her when she was eight and she still is angry. She remembers him climbing on her and her two sisters lying beside her in the bed and pretending to continue sleeping, denying with their bodies what was happening to her body. Now she has eight children by eight different men. She must go to classes, it has been ordered by the courts. She is a child abuser. She talks on.

Lupita eats daintily at her omelette. Her nails are polished, the body held with the certainty that men desire it. She begins to talk.

"His childhood? Yes, I knew him as a boy, I met him when he was nine, you know? They all lived on the side of a hill, Nacho had seven brothers and sisters, the mother, the stepfather—his natural father he was gone, prison maybe—and the mother and stepfather did not like Nacho. They would throw him down the hill—he would go flying through the air. Or the family would throw bricks at him, he would crouch and hold out his arms to protect himself and when the bricks hit, he would scream and yell. Nachito spent most of his time away from home, wandering Nogales, and when he came home, he was hungry and wanted to eat. You know? He was always hungry the way kids are. He had no shoes, no clothes, and he never attended school. I met his sisters when they were twelve or thirteen, they'd come to Tucson looking for work, you know. What kind? Oh, they would clean houses, like that. They had jumped the fence, you know."

Lupita almost mumbles when she talks of the charges against her for child abuse. They tell her in counseling sessions it goes back to the way she was raised. A brow arches, there is a faint smile that seems to say, *"Asi la vida."* She is very hungry, yet somehow manages to both devour her omelette and appear to pick at the slabs of cheese, ham, and egg.

I try to listen carefully but my mind drifts. The café is very new, the service noisy. I look out in the parking lot at new pickup trucks with chrome rollbars, at tires with white lettering, all the spoils of the trade. The decor is instant rustic, branding irons, cowboys on horseback in prints misty from the smoke off imaginary wood fires. The waitress wears a gingham blouse, tight jeans on generous hips. Lupita's voice does not vary, her eyes dart over to watch me from sentence to sentence. The eyes say, Why are you asking me this? What does it matter? They also say, Do you want me?

It is necessary to want her. She has had those eight children by eight different men. I must want her or she will not be able to keep talking. Her dyed hair has black roots, the eyes are well made up. I must want her. This is a common courtesy.

"What did he do? Did he read, watch television, drink hard?" I ask. "What did he do when he lived with you?"

She says, "He liked good clothes, liked being neat and clean. Sometimes he permed his hair so it would be just right. He didn't give his mother money. He spent it, I guess. He never had much money. He was not a heavy drinker. He had a good sense of humor, he laughed a lot and would always try to make people laugh.

"He wasn't bad-looking at all. If he had a woman, he would stay with her, he was a one-woman kind of man. He met this woman, back I think in 1981, and she was living with this black guy who wanted to marry her. He gave her nice rings and things. She lived in public housing. The guy found out about Nacho and he took everything back. Then Nacho started living with her, and she got pregnant, and they tossed her out of public housing. She was twenty-two. They had the baby, I was there at the delivery, and the baby was born with the fingers curled, I saw this, the fingers curled and one little finger sticking up—the baby was flinging the bird at the world. He was in prison when the baby was born—she's about seven now—and he never did see her.

"He'd get in fights with the mother. Once I was over there with a boyfriend and Nacho tried to shoot her with a rifle. He missed. He couldn't shoot you if you were just standing there. Once she got mad at him and took a swing at him and missed and smashed the aquarium and cut her arm bad. He wanted to kill her. I don't know, I guess he was mad at her.

"Religious? I was terrible myself about revenge and maybe that was why Nacho came to me. I was raped when I was young and I know if I could strike back I would never stop hitting. I think a lot of Nacho's killings were about his father, about striking back. You know they had a shootout back in 1980 or '81 in Nogales, he and his father, because Nacho said his father should help him and give him money, and his father refused, and Nacho said, you never felt for me when I was a boy or helped me, and his father said, how could I? I was in prison. And Nacho said, well, see, now I'm just like you.

"I had joined a new religion and Nacho would say, how can you do that, here have a cigarette, let's go drink, and after a while I thought, he's right, I should just be me.

"Nacho believed that he was born to die, that he wasn't going to like live forever. He didn't believe in God. I saw this big tattoo on his arm, just above the wrist, a spiral or something, just this big mess, like dirt, and I asked what is that thing, and he said, that's the Devil, the Devil doesn't have a form.

"Did he worship the Devil? Nacho wasn't the kind to worship nothing. He didn't have time for worship. He would die when he would die, when his time came.

"He didn't have friends. No, he didn't have friends. People were afraid of him. They knew who he was and what he did. He liked the United States better than Mexico. He said you could have a better life here. He said the prisons were better, you could get heat and air cooling and good food.

"That last day, the day he died, he was very nervous, walking back and forth in the room, looking outdoors. He had hardly had any sleep, he was working something out. He looked paranoid. He had to go meet someone. I heard he had a big argument with someone and that he and Carlos had a machine gun that night. They sent someone for the drugs for the deal. And then I don't know what happened."

She is staring at her plate of food, speaking so softly. It does not matter, don't you understand?

The call comes near midnight and the voice has a choking edge to it. She says the marriage has ended, thirteen years and the children, everything is over. The final decree comes down in the morning. The line is long distance and her voice weaves in and out of the electrical cracks of the night sky.

I am very tired and I do not have the right words of soothing emptiness at my command. A wooden vulture stares down from top of the television. I am lying on the floor. The remains of frozen dinners scold from the dirty carpet.

She says she knows it is better this way, she has had enough of the lying and cheating and the money disappearing. But thirteen years is kind of a habit, you know. She says she just needs someone to talk to. The night is a long, hard thing. She is halfway across the continent, the voice a tiny, spooked thing barely rasping through the receiver. I lean back with my head against the wall, the faint green paint stained with the dirt from my head, a smudged monument to similar calls. I can see her cat eyes, the generous breasts she is so proud of, the fierce hunger in her voice. She comes from a family where the women always devour the men, always. She comes from stock where the women never give up, never stop coming at you.

She has a job and that helps. It pays, the office is regular, the company fine. She is learning.

She says, "What are you doing?"

"Staring at the white tray remains of a microwave dinner."

"What kind?"

And I tell her and she is off. Christ, now she just goes to the supermarket, gets everybody the kind of dinner they want and it's so easy and everybody is happy, you know? What kind did you eat? Budget Gourmet? Sure, I get them, you gotta try the Veal Parmigiana and be sure and get one of those things that make them revolve, then you don't have to stop halfway through and turn the container around to make 'em cook evenly. Now you heard it here first, she says, be sure and get one.

The voice is picking up now, the size growing, the rasp spreading out like surf hitting a beach and becoming smooth, laughing, a sensuous strand. I am in the school of American cookery where she is off and running about memory, power settings, recall, the joys and horrors of digital clocks on the ovens—every time the power flutters the damn things lose it—and there is a mastery in her words. The woman teaching the man, the female leading the boy down the path to security and clean sheets. They are just little boys, her voice is saying.

Suddenly the words snap like a stick and she says she imagines things now, she imagines I will fly out, she will meet me at the airport. Sometimes she thinks she will be

wearing a coat and I will walk out of the door from the
passageway to the aircraft, leave that sunless metal tube
with the slant floor, worn carpet, machine air, and our
eyes will meet, she will hug me and step back and open her
coat. She will be wearing nothing. And I will lunge forward.

Other times, she imagines, I leave my plane and go to a
hotel. She knocks at the door and I open it. She is standing
there, well dressed and groomed. The nylons are perfect,
the shoes new and matching her gown, the scent off her
neck a drug. I invite her in. Her lips brush against mine, I
nibble at her neck. She gently pushes me aside, turns her
head ever so girlishly and asks me to sit down over there,
in that soft chair in the corner of the suite. The drapes
against the window will be closed, the room will have the
feel of a warm cave with just a glow of soft lighting. The
television will definitely not be on. She will tolerate no
distractions. Then with the faintest smile, almost a prim
smile, she disappears into the bathroom. I hear no pipes
singing, no bowls flushing. When she comes out, the lights
are still wonderfully low but one can see. She is wearing a
teddy, a cream-colored one, perhaps tending toward flesh
tones. Her breasts—honey, I've got great breasts—almost
spill from the lacy bodice and the crotch of the teddy has
snaps. She leans forward, a movement almost invisible to
the eye, and her cleavage grows dark and rich. My hand
will fumble, the snaps will pop open, I will roll the garment upward but not take it off. It is so much—it is better
if the silk is still against her body, she tells me. She tumbles backward and we will go very slowly. She has so
much to show, to teach, to experience. Her perfect teeth
bite my shoulder.

She has always been kind of inhibited, she says. The first
marriage, well, imagine coming home and finding your
husband in bed with your friend. And he beat her. And the
second one, well, he drank, and he had trouble and

blamed her, said awful things, and always insisted she go down on him. For hours.

But she is ready now. The teddy, honey, you'll have to see the teddy.

Her voice is lush, the words ooze through the phone. I say nothing, I am not needed. My head leans against the wall, I can feel the smudge growing like a flower. She must hang up now, we have been talking an hour. Tomorrow is the big day, honey. Thanks, she says, I'll be all right. And be sure you get one of those revolving trays and remember I told you. Remember.

I hear the click and then the peace of the dial tone. The wooden vulture stares down from atop the blank television screen. The head of the bird is red, then the white band, the tower of the black body. I picked it up in Mexico. It comforts me. The man in the market said that Indians made it. But when I sleep, the vulture is not present. I am in Mexico, to be sure, but her soft voice is flooding my mind and a scent rises up off her breasts. If I asked, asked even in a very quiet voice, I know she would get up from the bed, snap her teddy primly shut, and go into another room and cook me a fine dinner. She would tell me to be still, to let her take care of it. She is that kind of woman, a fine woman, a hungry woman.

Sometimes when she calls, she tells me she can read my mind, that she has felt that very day what was going through my brain. Her voice will be very affectionate when she says this. And then she will talk some more about the teddy, I must see the teddy.

> *Sometimes the words just don't come, because there is something holding them back. It don't do no good to just make something up. You can't say it if you don't feel it right. The words don't come. If you just say something to sound good, you might hurt somebody, or it might come back and hit you hard. You have to sit there and wait for it to come right out of your own body. Maybe it don't come.*

Then you know something is really wrong inside.
You can't force it out. You just have to try to live
right and then maybe it will come out of you some
other time.
                    —*Washoe speaker of the Native American*
                    Church [peyote], early 1950s

The phone messages pile up on my desk, little pink slips
demanding that words be spoken into the mouthpiece of a
machine. One is from Homicide. They are worried about
what Art and I are doing, they do not want us fucking up
their case. Some people stop talking to us on the south side
of town, their throats choked by the authorities. We agree
to meet.

The café in the motel is full of cops without uniforms.
They sit in clumps at the tables, white shirts, clipped hair,
trimmed moustaches, and beepers hang from their belts
like sacerdotal tools. The waitresses move coffee through
by the barrel, banter with the police. It is a lively, yet still
room. The voices are harsh but somehow manage to seem
subdued, certain, sure voices that knife words through the
air while maintaining the air of secret messages and special errands. I can feel the eyes boring into my back. Art
and I are the only civilians in the joint.

The man we are waiting for enters with a swagger and
immediately sits at our booth. Who else could we be? his
action seems to say, we sure as hell aren't cops. The curly
hair springs from his cocked head and immediately coffee
appears before him and he begins talking with a kind of
clear mumble, the words audible but the lips never moving. He wants to know what we know—Jesus Christ, this is
a homicide, you know, not some fucking game for the
press.

I tell him I don't think he really cares who killed Nacho.
What does it matter if the guys in the business whack each
other off?

He bridles at my remark. He is a cop, this is a case, he
solves cases. He fumes that he does care, that we do not

understand. I am off-balance for a moment. Men in the life disappear from the streets and then pop up dead in the desert all the time. And no one cares. I do not know why he is insisting this one killing matters and I am not going to find out. He is not here to reveal. His task is to deliver a message—Lay Off—and find out what, if anything, we have stumbled upon. His manner is not quite angry and not quite bored. It is the weariness of dealing with the straight world where no one knows what the fuck the real world is like.

"Nacho?" he explains. "He was just the help. Yeah, people around Nacho had machine guns, big guns. Not Uzis, they're too small now. Everyone's got a big gun these days. You feel kind of skinny out there with a .38. Hell, I've got a fucking machine gun in the trunk of my car.

"How much did Nacho take down? Oh, he could probably make a couple of grand a week when he wanted work.

"Killings? Who cares how many he killed? Ten, fifteen, more, what's it matter? For a guy like that, it doesn't mean anything. That's what he did: kill people. And anyway, those guys all brag, run up their scores. Right now, how many guys do you think are out there claiming they did Nacho?"

His eyes say he has a numbing idea of roughly how many dudes on the street currently claim the trophy.

He wants to get his background out of the way. Pay attention, his hands seem to say, as they knife the air. He has been a narc, been one for years, done deals in the scummiest parts of Nogales, gotten down with the boys. He knows the world that birthed Nacho. What the fuck, who cares? What the fuck has you so interested? he asks, and do you know what the fuck you're doing?

I sip coffee. His words, language firing from some machine gun in his throat, scatter around me. My mind drifts. Christ, I am sitting down with a narc, chatting up a storm with some son-of-a-bitch who made his living caging heads.

It is the fall of 1967, I drive a white MGA, top down, her red hair flutters in the wind. We stop at a liquor store and buy a corkscrew and a bottle of good French wine. She knows her vineyards.

We drive west into the foothills of the Tucson mountains, the desert flows around us dark and thick as paste. The pavement ends, gravel grinds under the wheels, and houses tacked onto the acres fall away. I turn the machine around and park, the city spreads before us a carpet of lights. We talk, drink wine, savor being young in an aging world that goes nowhere or to Vietnam. I am 1-A and using up my time with hard drives, strong drink, and other aids.

She has never had a joint and, luck being what it is, she has tumbled onto a messiah for any substance that will tear the mind into new pieces that confound a nine-to-five future. I get out and walk back to the trunk where a half a pound of grass rests in little baggies, a New Age wine cellar. We light up, the sweet smoke curls into the night, and our brains lift off. She notices the bright colors of the lights below and all the usual symptoms follow. We make love on the hood of the car.

I start the engine and we drive down into town, the wine bottle clutched in my hand. At the bend of Miracle Mile a cop pulls us over. We are drunk, stoned, and there is that half pound of grass pursuing us in the trunk. I get out, talk to him, and he lets us go. There is never an explanation for these moments of grace.

There are other moments but always they are the same. I have drugs, they have the law. Friends get busted, the usual legal mortar attacks of the period. Narcs. The mind police of the state.

And now I listen to one and feel nothing at all. I have aged but so has the country. Art and I have snapshot memories of the fifties and sixties and seventies. Part of the distance between my happy joint and Nacho is hidden somewhere in those black and white freeze frames. It is the mid-1950s and for a narc like Art, Tucson's drug scene is compact: forty or fifty heroin or opium addicts, and the business is concentrated in Barrio Libre between Broadway, 17th Street, Stone Avenue, and Main, in Old Pasqua Village off Miracle Mile and over in El Rio. The addicts are the dealers. It is 1965 and a friend of mine walks around the University of Arizona with a briefcase full of LSD that he peddles, like a Fuller Brush man, in the dorms. It is the early seventies, there is a construction slowdown, and a bunch of out-of-work bricklayers try to find some money. The door of the trailer opens at night, and I stand there with an exquisite scale for weighing random samples of the wares. The truck with the load is due within the hour, and instantly everyone shoulders a shotgun or a rifle. It is June 1987, the door opens on a shed in south Tucson and there stands the man surrounded by two thousand pounds of marijuana. You want twenty pounds? I've got it today, I don't know about tomorrow. Art is dazzled by the neat stacks and the aroma of money, power, and drugs.

In the first six months of the year, 4,400 pounds of coke were seized in southern Arizona. No one knows what is going on, but the numbers strike a chord. In 1985, the cops took down eighty-five pounds of coke in the state. In 1986, their score ran to 2,706, in '87 5,070. By '88, they'll bag 10,000 pounds. Things change, I tell myself, things change. And so do I.

The cop is flying now, determined to teach us what we need to know. He realizes we are fools, Boy Scouts in a hard game. His hands reach into the creamer bowl and he starts placing little sealed capsules of the stuff around on the formica tabletop. Each capsule represents a different police force in Nogales, Sonora.

"Now," he begins with a withering contempt, "the Burned Ones control this set of cops, Caro Quintero controls this other set of cops, and so forth. Now, I'm not talking about local punks. I'm talking about the guys you read about all the time, the guys from way down south, the big guys. Not all the cops are crooked—it would be unfair to say that. There's some honest guys down there and I don't want you smearing the cops in Nogales, got it? Okay.

"But be careful. Never, never, never go to the Federales for information, you understand? Don't even think about it. They all wear silk shirts, the Rolex watches, and they drive fleets of stolen American cars for their personal use. Fuck, I mean, don't even think about going to the station. People go in there and never come out. Look, when I'm down there on official business, I sure as hell never go there."

School is about out. He stabs our blank faces with questions and decides we don't know shit. Promises are made to keep in touch. Hell, come down to the station and I'll show you the file. That kind of thing. Of course, this will never happen and we both know it.

I stare off into the sterility of the room full of cops talking about cases they will make. Outside the freeway whirs with traffic and smog lifts into the morning sky. They are players in a hopeless game and they treasure this futility and insist everyone share it. The cop has one more message before he lets us slip away into our innocence and ignorance.

"Hey," he says, "next time you're down there ask about El Chinnok, the Canadian. These two Canadian guys went down to Nogales, you see, fronting for a big deal back home. They tried to pull something off, tried to get behind the deal. The Mexicans in Nogales tied El Chinnok to a tree. Then they pried his eyes out with a beer can opener, tortured him a while, and finally shot him. They made his partner watch. Then they turned him loose and said,

hey, go back and deliver the message."
    School is over.

It is midnight at the office and I stare into the black and white computer screen watching words magically appear on the screen. My hands are cold, I have not eaten for a day, and my belly spins from a dozen shots of tequila tossed down in various Nogales saloons. I cradle a cup of coffee in my hand and listen to the purring of the air-conditioning system. No one else is here, this is the sweet time. A stuffed cloth trout hangs from the ceiling and keeps company with a rubber bat. On the wall photos of my son, the face fat with contentment, look down on me.

    I am pounding out notes, quotes, clues, little bits of the debris of the drug world. I want to go to bed but I cannot. I write for hours. I look at the kid's pictures and can hear him babbling. I am convinced that something like syntax is beginning to appear in his sounds and snorts, the emergence of sentences and all the arguments to follow. His eyes are fresh and ready to find some images.

    I pull down an old manuscript and stare dumbly at the pages. I collect quotes that never find a home, nails driven into my brain that ache but make no sense when displayed to others. When I was a boy I curled up on the floor and read about the wild, free West, the place of possibilities. George Catlin led me to this fantasy. He was a so-so painter of Indian portraits who toured the nation peddling his vision of the back-of-the-beyond. Sometimes he had wild Indians along in those decades before the Civil War as he reported on the darkest dreams of his audience. I flip to a long quote from his book, *Adventures of the Ojibbeway and Ioway Indians in England, Belgium and France,* a text published in 1852. His prose is very antiquated to my ear, full of long clauses suspended in air by commas, semicolons, and other semaphores of a kind of nonhuman speech. The incident he embalms occurs in the autumn of 1844. I can hear this clear, educated voice pointing out the whimsy and silliness of life. A safe, sure voice that knows the future and knows it will be good and secure and worth having for everyone.

When the poor untutored Indians, from the soft and simple prairies of Missouri, seated themselves upon a beam, and were looking into and contemplating the immensity of a smoking steeping-vat, containing more than 3000 barrels, and were told that there were 130 others of various dimensions in the establishment—that the edifice covered twelve acres of ground, and that there were necessarily constantly on hand in their cellars 232,000 barrels of ale, and also that this was only one of a number of breweries in London, and that similar manufactories were in every town in the kingdom, though in less a scale, they began, almost for the the first time since their arrival, to evince profound astonishment. . . . The pipe was lit and passed around while they got, in the meantime, further information of the wonderful modes and operations of this vast machine; and also, in round numbers, read from a report by one of the proprietors, the quantity of ale consumed in the kingdom annually. Upon hearing this, which seemed to cap the climax of their astonishment, they threw down the pipe, and leaping into an empty vat, suddenly dissipated the pain of their mental calculations by joining in the Medicine (or Mystery) Dance. Their yells and screaming echoing through the vast and vapouring halls, soon brought some hundreds of maltsmen, grinders, firers, mashers, ostlers, painters, coopers, et al., peeping through and amongst the blackened timbers and casks, and curling and hissing fumes, completing the scene as the richest model for the infernal region.

I pound on until about twelve, then hit a bar for one more drink to shut me down. Everything is so tidy on the sheets of paper, all the symbols in a row, all the rows in order. I can smell the raw sewage of the Colonia Buenos

Aires but the slap of the wine on my tongue overwhelms this flicker of memory.

The Colonia Buenos Aires sits right by the fence, just over the hill from downtown Nogales, Sonora. The entrance, a narrow street, knifes between two hills, the surface rutted, people walking everywhere with bags of food in their hands, the gateway a perfect bottleneck. Once inside, the district opens up and houses and dirt streets tumble up and down the hills of an interior basin. Streets signs are few, the whole place a maze. Here and there *cholos* stand around smoking and looking up with empty eyes.

The light is good, the temperature around 100 degrees. Messages shout from the walls: CHUKOS POBRES, COMMUNISMO. The homes are largely brick and block, the windows have glass, the yards boast flowers here and there, and the district does not have the feel of grinding poverty—no cardboard shacks, no windowless hovels. Up a side street, a goat browses by a fallen grocery cart and a woman stands in a long red skirt watering some plants with a hose. Her face says there are no clocks here.

I lean against Art's truck and drink in the scene. I have been here often before in many cities. In Chicago it was Lawndale with the Conservative Vice Lords hugging the sidewalk and parting ever so slowly as I walk through, the only white face in a sea of black. A block away a Chicago bank with Greek columns stands lonely, the empty hulk gutted by the flames of the last revolt. Across the street, vacant lots mark where a war had toppled tenements, apartment houses once filled with striving Jews in the 1920s and '30s. I am in an American Berlin but no one speaks German and the Allied bombers are grounded at the moment. The faces are totally passive, the lips unmoving, the eyes blank. But everything says the same thing every time and every place: Wait until dark.

Some yards are fenced with big dogs prowling behind

the wire. The grocery stands across from the burying ground, a weed-strewn block of monuments called *Pantheon de los Heroes.* Nacho rots in that place, at least for a while. When you no longer can pay for your grave, they dig you up and pitch the bones away. This is the home ground. The head of the Burned Ones is said to be building a castle here, complete with moat. Once they raid his house, find no one at home, blood on the walls, and a nice van with custommade gun slits. A child walks by, her schoolbox sporting a drawing of men on the moon. The kids wear T-shirts that report VOTE NO . . . OTT YMCA TUCSON ARIZONA . . . MICKEY MOUSE. A hundred yards or more to the north, Gringolandia begins. A car rolls past with a loudspeaker on the roof blaring the day's news: a bad car crash up around Casa Grande, Arizona.

Rio Hondo, the street where Nacho was raised, is almost vertical, water trickling down the center of the track. A woman stands in the middle of the road, her dress red, stockings a heavily patterned black net, the heels high and also black. Her lips are pursed, deep red, and moist. She stares into the dirt and appears to notice nothing. The United States is a football pass away.

A Coca-Cola truck unloads cases of soft drinks, children laugh and run by. There is nothing out of the ordinary, there never is. It is a place where people live and make whatever kind of life they can. In Nogales itself there have been one hundred forty murders in the past six months. This among a population of 200,000. In the Colonia, one small scab among many in the community, there have been a half-dozen killings in the last month. The police have the photos—hands tied behind backs, slashes with the knife. Cigarette burns dancing across the still flesh. The business demands these moments of discipline. I look into the faces of the children, brown moons with eyes that seek life.

Later, the cops say, with mock surprise, "You went into

Buenos Aires? That is a den of wolves."

The night comes down.

Lupita stares down into her eggs and remembers the house on the dirt street in Buenos Aires and thinks. "The house was four rooms, small but nice. They had an indoor toilet, you know." The local newspaper, *La Voz del Norte*, skips this "Leave It to Beaver" talk and takes a shot at Nacho: "Since he was very little, he had demonstrated that he was a sociopath who killed for any minor offense; others have indicated that he was a product of the age in which he happened to be born on this border, a product of the decade of the sixties."

The Mexican cop offers simply a folk poetry. His sheet begins:

IGNACIO ROBLES VALENCIA (A) EL NACHITO ROBLES—born December 14, 1959, in Nogales, Sonora; his siblings are LUIS, MANUEL, RITA, ISABEL, ANTONIO, OLGA AND HUMBERTO on Rio Hondo No. 372.... His parents are IGNACIO ROBLES MORALES AND PETRA VALENCIA GARCIA. His height is 5'7", his weight 145 pounds, thin, dark brown complexion, nose medium, mouth medium, lips regular, flaring nostrils, oval chin, black wavy hair, brown eyes, thick straight eyebrows, thin moustache (trimmed), clean shaven, regular forehead, free citizen of the state, unemployed, and he has the following visible marks: ON HIS RIGHT CHEEK HE HAS TWO SCARS, ON THE RIGHT ARM A TATTOO OF A FACE, ON HIS LEFT ARM A PEACOCK, ON HIS CHEST THE HEAD OF A TIGER, A ROSE, A SPIDER WEB AND SPIDER, ON HIS BACK THE VIRGIN OF GUADALUPE AND THE FACE OF A WOMAN.

Then there is the matter of his brother. In May, a month after Nacho became a sack of bones and rot, another murder boiled out of Nogales. A man in Colonia Buenos Aires is said to have made comments about Nachito and the brother then shot and killed the man. The Mexican police deny this. The Tucson cops are skeptical also. It is talk, they say to us, many killings are just talk, bullshit, brag, you know?

I lean against the wooden bar of a Sonoran saloon a couple of blocks from Buenos Aires and the barkeep says, "Of course it is true." I look up at the huge back bar with its fine polished mirrors and see tourists laughing and talking. There is a table full of women from the University of Arizona's archeological museum. One comes over and says hello and we talk of the wonderful basket collection that documents the early people in these parts. She smiles broadly and is ready for a fine day of sunshine, booze, and food in another country.

I turn back to the barkeep, a man of quick wits and good instincts. The door of joint advises that no guns and uniforms are allowed. I make inquiry about this bit of etiquette. Mariachis are playing and the man is very hard to hear. He leans forward into my face and Art cranes his neck to catch the splatter of border Spanish on the fine varnished bar top. The speaker is from Buenos Aires and he is angry.

"The cops are worse than the crooks," he spits. "A few days ago, a couple of them came in here with their pistols dangling and I sent one of the guys working tables over and told them to cover their weapons. They told him to go to hell. So I went over. They said, 'You want trouble?' I told them, what do I care, kill me, what's the difference. I haven't got any family, so what do I have to worry about?"

His face is stretched tight as he talks, the bones and skin signaling this is not happy chat from the man pouring the drinks. The mariachis bathe his words with chords of good cheer. His eyes go black and I think they are a deep well I may fall into.

"Nacho?" he snaps. "Sure I knew Nacho, know the family. No, I'm not going to talk about him. He's dead, but his family isn't, his gang isn't. Just when you think you're the best—and he was the best—that's when they kill you."

He walks down the line pouring drinks and laughing

with customers. There will be no more talk here.

Art and I continue to drink. We are on different missions in a way. Art is still pretending to be making a case, building shreds of evidence bit by bit so that the bust can come down, the D.A. will smile with contentment, the bad guy will sit in a cell and know he has been had, outfoxed, nailed cold and clean. There is little or no money in this case for him. Of course, he insists on money, he must have an excuse for himself, but what he is being paid will hardly cover the gas, much less the drinks. He is easy to dismiss as the old cop who cannot give up his habits. But this logic does not touch his motives. This I sense. He keeps his reasons hidden from me, he easily breaks out into hollow diatribes against the drug traffic, the criminals, the menace. But like most hunters, his only real love is his prey. And now he once again hunts what he loves. In the end, his Nacho cannot be a sociopath or psychopath or simply a criminal. His Nacho is an *hombre,* a man who would not stay down. It is not important that he failed, that he died like a dog. Failure is part of the life, a key part of the life that flows through Art's veins. Mexico is full of statues of defeated generals. I think of a story Art once told me, about a pistolero on the south side, a man who runs a good piece of action, moves some decent-sized loads. He is about thirty, and they say on the street he has millions. He wears tight Levis, the shirt open in the front, the gold chains, blank, impassive face. There is a detail about him that he keeps bringing up. The man is said to keep a house on the south side and the place is stocked with a half-dozen women. When he goes there—and who is to say when that will be? when the mood strikes him—they meet him at the door, unbutton his pants, go down on him. *Hombre.* He has not bowed down to life, he has not given in, he has not been polite. Of course, he will die, be another body by the road. But he will have lived. Just as Nacho lived. And so Art hunts his man.

My own purposes are vague, but my standards much

lower, my expectations more negotiable. I want to know where Nacho comes from and how he became what he was the night he died in the warm spring desert at a drug deal that went the other way. I want to feel the emptiness in his belly, and then sense the warm glow as he feeds and feels, however briefly, full and content. We argue about the work but it is a waste of time. We are speaking different languages. I know I will never get inside Ignacio Robles Valencia, I will simply examine his footprints, smell his spoor on the streets of Nogales, see his image in the dark eyes of the living who are still afraid to speak of this particular dead man. But I hope, sometimes suspect, I will feel the yearning within him, before he is embalmed with the clinical language we use to kill the disorderly, the distasteful, the threatening. The bad.

It is time to go to the state police station. According to the cop in Tucson who lectured over the coffee creamers, this particular force is in the pocket of the Burned Ones, a local drug gang spun off two reckless brothers. A few months back one the brothers was in a whorehouse in Nogales and started arguing with another guy. He then left, went to his car, and suddenly reappeared in the doorway. He hosed down the bar with a machine gun. Then there was the time he killed a guy, then showed up at the burial and circled the cemetery in a car shouting obscenities.

The station is a block off the main drag of Nogales. A half-dozen men stand around the horses smoking and laughing, automatic rifles dangling from their hands. They wear the dress of vaqueros and stare with the eyes of cops. The morning light plays off their faces as they examine the battered car—front wheel buckled under like a broken leg, glass shattered. The click of typewriters flows out the open windows of the Nogales police station and two uniformed cops survey the street from the door, hands resting on their .45s.

The head cop's office has more typewriters, the windows

open, the June heat pouring through and there is no cooling system. Everyone wears good shoes, an easy smile, and hard eyes. Outside in the lobby people cool their heels. Some basketball players from Utah come in. They had parked their van by the Nogales railroad station, gotten on the train for a vacation, and now they are back and their van has been broken into and ransacked and another car of theirs is missing. This will be difficult, the police explain, we must have your registration, proof of ownership. But the papers are in the missing car, the Americans explain. Shrug, what can we do, then? One of the cops is driving the missing car, it is outside the building. How can we return it without the proper papers?

Outside on the balcony of the building is a mural made of tiles: a pirate holds a sword over his head, his other arm clutches a beautiful woman, her blouse torn and one breast exposed, and at their feet is booty.

Two guys are brought in handcuffed. They are spirited to a small closet with no windows and no air, plopped into two chairs, and left to think. The door is closed on them. After a while a cop opens the door, the two guys are drenched with sweat. The cop walks up to one and feints a blow with one hand, the prisoner raises his arms to ward it off, and then the cop cracks him cleanly on the chin with his other fist. He abruptly turns and leaves, shutting the door. As he passes the clerk in the lobby, he says, "They're not ready yet."

The police know of El Nacho. Yes, they smile, he was *El Famoso*. The father, oh yes, El Bronco, a gun smuggler, robber. Killer? Perhaps.

We have been told that Nacho did work for the police, little assignments. So did his father. There is a book in Spanish that gives clues, a small volume by one Jorge Issachtts Corrales, a convict, entitled *Volvere a vivir (I Will Return to Live)*. The text, a cloud of words drifting like pain across the page, sputters out this: "Observation: Monday, March 4, 1974. Time? 12:35 approximately. . . . It is important to clear up who killed Ramon Rendon Amparano. . . . Isn't it true, Warden, even though you didn't order it yourself, that this killing was done by your paid pistolero Ignacio Robles Moreles [Nacho's natural father]? Wasn't it also this same gentleman during other investigations who shot [a list of names]. . . ."

We do not mention this testament to the cops. One is especially friendly after a while. Something seems to click between us. His boss explains that due to confidentiality and the rights of citizens it would be impossible for us to see the records. The friendly one takes us down into the patio—the police station once was the home of wealthy doctor, a man who apparently made one big mistake—across the cement, past shiny cars that have been confiscated, and into the records section of the outfit.

Yes, the man smiles, they have some records—they know of four killings El Nacho did in Nogales, plus two more they are certain he did. How many in all? Go to Hermosillo, go to San Luis, check Tucson, Phoenix, Mesa. There are many records. Who knows?

The sheets are pulled on El Nacho, a string of robberies for violence, of murders. His father, El Bronco, also has a sheet—drunk and disorderly, arms smuggling, all the little moments interspersed with long silences when he was in prison. El Nacho's face peers from an old mugshot, he is fifteen in the picture.

We take the photograph with us. No one ever asks for a bribe. Ever. We have slipped into a zone beyond simple commerce.

I want out, the friendly cop says maybe this evening we can meet and talk, but I want out. I sense something I cannot state, and it tells me to go, now. Art says, let's visit my relative, and we go deeper into the town where his people own a truckstop. The man is all smiles when we enter, beer appears, and he says, "Nacho? Certainly, I know of Nacho. My friend the commandante can tell you much about him. I will call him now." A few moments later, he returns, "Ah," he says, "the commandante is not in office at this moment, but he is said to be returning later."

No matter, he remembers one story the commandante told him.

"My friend, the commandante," he explains, "he was once in San Luis when Nacho got out of prison. Well, the commandate remembers Nacho walking out the gate and seeing these two guys just standing there doing nothing. He decks them both and then smiles, kind of like he slugged the guys just to flex his muscles."

Afterwards, you rue the fact that you've been so kind.
—*Adolf Hitler, April 27, 1945,*
three days before he perished in his bunker

A former Mexican president once said, "All friends are false, all enemies are real." I will never know Mexico. It is beyond my range.

I am in a city below the capital struggling to learn elementary Spanish. I am failing. My maestro lives in a two-story house with cool tile floors. Below the balcony, a small garden thrives and when the rains pause, the volcano stares down on the fields of Morelos. My teacher is thirty-four, owner of his own language school. He is dark and smart, and has married a Swiss.

Even with the collapse of the economy he lives well. Of course, he and the wife now must manage a small hotel on the side and take boarders into their home to make ends meet. She smiles all the time and his black eyes are always brooding. He favors American rock 'n' roll or the new British records. Once a week, a small dark man comes and does the yard. He crawls across the grass cutting it with hedge clippers. The Swiss wife watches from the kitchen window where she is busy boiling their drinking water. Next door lives an architect, his house a small jewel, the backyard centered on a swimming pool. Just down the block some Indians have commandeered a vacant lot and build a shanty. Chickens scratch in the dirt, the wood fire wisps smoke into the warm evening, and naked kids look blankly as I walk past. In the evening, adolescent boys gather in the street and dance to American music in tight knots of energy.

Each day for lunch I cut across a small park on my way home from school. The little square of green is full of men mowing the lawn, all down on their haunches wielding blades which they sharpen with rocks. They work three days on the small park, making the thing last. When I walk past they look up with black eyes and never miss a stroke sharpening their blades.

I am ambling up the street to my maestro's house, my head knocking out the conjugation of *conocer.* An old Indian woman hobbles past, the leather face all wrinkles, the dress a long rag almost reaching the ground. I have seen her begging up at the plaza, her eyes scanning the swaying hips of the women scurrying past on high heels. She stops ahead, squats, and a hot puddle flows right out of her in front of my maestro's house.

I'll never know Mexico. It is beyond my range.

Grackles yell from the trees on the plaza and people circle the public square savoring the warm night. The cafés bask under yellow lights and men smoke and drink beer and eat shrimp. Taxis wait patiently for customers, children squeal and romp. Night caresses San Blas, a community of 7,000 people between the sea and jungle in the Mexican state of Nayarit, 1,200 miles south of the border. Father Junípero Serra used this town in 1768 as a jumping-off point for California and Alaska, the mother mission for a tactical strike by the cross against the pagan West. A ruined fort and a ruined church sleep tonight above the town on a rock promontory. Strangler vines and mahogany trees pry the old blocks apart with probes of their hungry roots.

Originally the place belonged to Huichol Indians, a shy group these days usually sighted as emblems on the favorite local hot sauce. Tonight there is Billy. We enter a small café for a drink and there he is. He slumps over his table, his beard run wild, hair slicked back, the skin on his face taut. He smokes and sips a beer and little veins etch all the yesterdays across his eyes. He says he came down here last winter because he hates the cities and this winter, well, he stopped in Tucson to see a friend and the cops came through the windows because his friend was, well, you know, holding. So he drifted down to San Blas again.

He has been around, he says. Nam. Around.

A room at the El Dorado sets him back about three bucks a day and what the hell, so the toilet seat is missing. He's got an idea, jewelry, big yellow stones. He'll start up a factory down here, sell the stuff in the States. Easy money, he says, smacking his lips. The American dream lives amid the jungle. Billy does not look up as he speaks and his voice seems to ride a monorail. He stopped getting excited a long time ago, way back before the checks started arriving every month and pensioned him off from American society.

It's the noise in the city, he says, too much sound. He can't take the roar. In the city, he whispers, everything sounds like incoming.

Look at these people, he murmurs, and his eyes sweep the busy plaza. No television, he explains, they got nothing else to do, so they come to the plaza.

He whips out a small book of Spanish phrases as evidence of his serious intentions in San Blas. He will devote at least the whole winter to his residence here. He will learn the language. The jewelry factory, that too will take up his time.

"How can anyone leave here?" he asks.

He sips beer for about twenty-five cents American and a shrimp dinner sets him back a buck or so. The peso continues its crazy death dance and things just get better and better for Billy.

We stand and leave and head for the hotel six blocks off the plaza. A room for two overlooking the harbor and convenient to the swimming pool, bar, and restaurant, all for less than six bucks a day.

Dinner is being served, first fruit salad with melon, pineapple, mango, watermelon; then shrimp, rice, bread, and salad. Flan for dessert. The waitress, possibly fourteen, glides over the tile floor in a state of grace as coconut palms whisper in the night breeze outside.

Then to our room. The tile floors feel cool to the feet, the sliding doors open to the balcony. The tide races into the estuary and past the breakwater, the lights of small fishing vessels flicker.

No commercial flights land in San Blas. The town is two hours by bus from Tepic and three or four hundred miles from the big port of Mazatlán. The insects are fierce much of the year. The hotels have no televisions or radios or cooling systems in the rooms. One bar in town has air conditioning and when I enter, the joint is empty. Downtown there are no magazines in English and no newspapers in any language.

We stand on the balcony drinking the night air like a drug. We have arrived inside one of those colorful magazine advertisements of a tropical vacation. She will spend each day on the beach listening to the waves break and tanning a nice brown. We will stroll village lanes amid the chatter of friendly peasants. I will forget work. We will revive passion. These things are all implicit in the advertisements and now we await the delivery of what we have bought. Outside a green harbor light spins and gleams as ocean sounds pour through the doorway into the cool, dark room.

Of course, we meet people.

She is very blond, he is brown with a black beard. Their time here is almost ended. They say the waves begin in the spring and run through October, great waves, some a mile long, waves that have made the *Guinness Book of Records*. Just to the south at Matanchen Bay, the waves break to the right and the left.

"A perfect right and left," he testifies.

He bends down and draws the play of the ocean in the dirt and then smiles approvingly at his diagram of tumbling water. He has been surfing fifteen years, nine right here in San Blas. His wife has been at it five years. They have a house in Mazatlán and one here. He does not explain his income. When the ocean goes flat here in November, they will head south along the coast hunting better water. He says people come to San Blas from all over the planet for the waves, people from Asia, Europe, the United States, from all over. The summers are very bad. It rains and it is hot and the mosquitoes and "no-see'ums"—*jejenes*—devour the flesh. The surfers stay in the water and even then are tortured by insects. The beaches are deserted. He boasts that only surfers, butterfly collectors, and bird watchers can endure the summers of San Blas.

She says, "You must have a strong reason to be here, or you'll move on."

Her shoulders are broad from the sport, her hips narrow. The body has been sculpted by the waves. Her mane of blond hair blazes against the lush green tropical leaves and vines.

They laugh that every few years someone tries to make San Blas click as a resort. Down on the beach, they say, is a monster hotel built in 1951 by addled Mexican businessmen. It was abandoned years ago. Now some more businessmen from the capital, Tepic, plot how to reopen it and they have workmen toiling over the gutted hulk. These notions spring up like plants after the summer rains. There is even talk of a Holiday Inn landing in San Blas. The two surfers dismiss these ambitions. Nothing, they are confident, can override the bugs. They advise us that after a few years you adjust and no longer get a welt from the bites.

As they speak they stand in the early morning light by a wall of green bamboo, smiling and swatting themselves and talking about the waves of summer.

We walk down to the beach to see the old hotel that is being renovated. A barefoot Mexican man rides his bicycle through the lobby and hops off on the veranda where others cook meat and boil coffee over a wood fire. Several men rake and chop around the grounds which have gone wild. Some harvest coconuts from the palms lining the patio. The first floor has been neatly whitewashed.

The three-story Hotel Hermosa rests by the sea with empty windows seeping rust from ancient wounds. No glasses clink in the gutted bar and furniture fashioned from thick wooden slabs waits for guests in the big lobby. On the wall, Father Junípero Serra stalks a miracle in a painting. The place spins me back to the 1950s and I cannot escape the notion that everything I am seeing should be in black and white. Erroll Flynn should be leaning against the bar, a hot Latin woman by his side, and a combo filling the air with salsa sounds. The owner will be fat, dressed in a suit, with a pencil thin moustache and big smile. He is telling Flynn how honored he is to have him in his establishment and is there anything he can provide?— Girls? Yes, we have girls! Flynn, strung out on speed, is busy dousing the flames in his liver with tequila, and his eyes, half hooded, take in the place with boredom but what the hell, everything is being comped so that he'll spread the word to his Hollywood friends.

The woman at his side wears a dress that reveals deep cleavage and she speaks with a bewitching accent. Her makeup is perfect, the face an oval with eyes steaming from black craters of mascara. She smiles broadly, and her hips jut out. She is the center of attention, she believes, and must run with the star's aura of macho. Up in the room, he falls asleep in his drunkenness but she will not reveal this fact.

I turn and the colors come back, Flynn is gone but then he was never here anyway. The saint still glares out from the painting, a nasty-looking fellow who is off to California where he will flog Indians, herd them into concentration camps he will call missions, watch his communicants drop dead from plagues, and hope some day to be canonized. Outside broken glass bottles top a wall. The workers move here and there, an army restoring a pyramid. Beyond the patio, past another low white wall, steers browse in the brush near the sea. Groove-billed anis, long-tailed black birds with thick, lined beaks, follow the beasts through the brush and feed on the fat ticks drinking the warm blood of the cattle.

We stroll back to the center of town. *"Señor Chicken es Magnifico,"* announces the sign at the live poultry stall in the market. Three metal chutes hang over a tin gutter. A fourteen-year-old boy lifts a leghorn from the pen and pitches the bird upside down over the chute so that only his head hangs into the generous funnel. Then with a quick flick of the blade he slits the bird's throat and blood trickles and runs down before spilling onto the floor. The bird rolls its eye at the afternoon market, blood flows a brilliant red against the white feathers. Other chickens in the nearby pen feed and cluck and do not look up.

In time, we meet other visitors. Marta and Mike are from Kansas and they think it is the water. They are sleeping ten hours a day and want still more. Miles from town in the jungle is a freshwater spring, La Tovora, and they visited this place on a boat ride. Their guide stopped his motor, they slipped into their suits, and dove into the bubbling water. Marta says it had a special feel, an ease to it. She says you have to get in the water and drink it, lots of it. And then you slow down, just like San Blas itself. This whole town, she argues, is sleepwalking and it is all because of the water.

She is sitting on the hotel balcony right now, touting the water and the calm of San Blas. She is a heavy woman, but still vivacious and attractive. It is not that she carries her weight well, it is that you cannot see her fat. She is a force, blond, smiling, alive. Back home, she explains, the banks are gobbling up the farms and there is not a lot of calm. She and Mike live in the Flint Hills and a neighbor went to the local bank and said, "I know I'm going to lose the farm but can I keep the house? Just the house? It has been in my family five or six generations."

"The home place," Marta intones like a prayer.

The bank said no.

So the neighbors took all the man's equipment, his tractors, combines, balers, you name it, and hid them on their own farms. But the bank hired a helicopter and hunted the stuff down. Then the bank held an auction and all the neighbors showed up and nobody was allowed to bid except local people, and they'd bid maybe a buck for a $50,000 tractor, a buck and a half for a combine. The bank said, well, you can keep the house.

"Banks are mean," Marta says. Her face for an instant is hard, cruel Kansas winters beat against it and contort the soft lines and generous eyes. She is the woman of the plains, a warm creature facing a land that withers everything. Then she looks out to sea and ease floods her once again. It is the water, like she says. "Wheat's shot," she erupts, "and cattle are down. Some people are growing Flint Hills sensimilla." Mike laughs.

They have a big satellite dish back at the farm and the thing sucks up everything in North America. When "Night Line" comes on they can even get to see people in the

Green Room waiting for their moment on camera. They are amazed at how folks will chat and be friendly with each other backstage and then come out and holler at each other on television. But the most amazing thing of all, Mike thinks, is that they get hundreds of television stations now and every time he flips through the channels he finds that *Clockwork Orange* is on somewhere. Imagine, he says, a country where someone at any time of the day or night is watching *Clockwork Orange.*

We have a beer, frigate birds wheel above. Marta relaxes and repeats, "It's the water."

Flickers of energy periodically punch through the heavy tropical air of the town. A parade sweeps by with legions of children, the girls waving banners, the boys bearing wooden guns and machetes. Teachers shout commands and stomp their high heels to the military drumbeat. The small army moves along under the banana trees and tall palms. Here and there bougainvilleas flare with color. The children chant, "Hola! Hola!" and then they are gone. After they pass, a pig wanders down the street searching for the slops of San Blas.

In time, we begin to stir from our slumbers and decide we must see the birds. Smoke wafts off smoldering coconut husks in the doorways as yellow-winged caciques scream overhead. At 5:00 A.M. clouds of insects own San Blas. The day begins with howls blasting from the brass horns of the tiny navy base as Mexican sailors spring to reveille. The streets are dotted with clumps of sleeping dogs and here and there a hog scratches and pokes in the rubbish. The tortilla factory opens off the plaza and people line up for a stack. Men wait for rides, trucks unload at the market, and one café opens early and offers beer, tequila, and black coffee. The plaza ripples with muscle as men wielding machetes stream out into the jungle and the work.

I am emerging from a fog. The days have washed some

tension from my body. I go to bed without strong drink, sleep hard, awaken at first light. I notice birds, go nowhere without my guidebook. A trogon stares down from a branch and for the first time in months it matters to me. I stop seeing things as stories, inches, picas, points. My ears open, I hear her voice, the laughter in it, and realize poison is dripping from my body, rolling down my skin like sweat and splashing silently to the floor. The flowers, my God, the flowers are huge with color and fat with scent. I am convinced I have escaped my world for some other place where nothing really happens or ever matters. The town does have seven thousand people but I insist on viewing it as a village, a human community subtly organized, a place of harmony and gay festivals. We go to an old hotel off the plaza, the bar is rustic and a stuffed crocodile holds court. The courtyard is an amiable half ruin, the style of Mexico in the tropics, and vines splatter against the walls. The fog is lifting.

Manuel waits by the bridge on the edge of town. Egrets fish the shallow waters and men huddle over smoky fires seeking an escape from the insects. The line casts off, the motor starts, and we glide upstream into the mangrove and *marismas* (Savannahs).

Manuel shouts, "Look, look, a boat-billed heron. Very unusual. Very."

A gawky bird stands on a limb with a bill copied from a steam iron. Warblers dart through the green wall of leaves and trees chatter with cries and songs. San Blas is the bird center of western Mexico. Here the jungle and the forest collide with the sea, birds from all three habitats mingle, hundreds of species of birds. Parrots and parakeets are the main draw, white-fronted parrots, blue-rumped parrotlets, and so forth. Green swarms of birds drift over the town and into the jungle, chattering above as they move toward food.

Manuel Lomeli is the only man in San Blas who knows

the birds. His English is fluent, and his ear and eye for birds encompass some four hundred species. He has spent eighteen years on the river, the past twelve studying the birds. At first, he would take people out for tours of the jungle and some of them would insist he stop, and then they would stare up into the trees with binoculars.

"I wondered what in the hell they were doing," he says.

He found out. First he pestered people with questions, and then some of them gave him bird guides. Finally, he laid hands on some binoculars. He is about forty, solid, and has a brooding presence. The patter of the San Blas boat guide seems to have been erased from his manner, and he is now the student of ornithology, the *hombre* who knows the birds.

The boat stops dead in the water and Manuel bursts into bird song.

"I think," he whispers, "there's a golden vireo in there."

Our eyes scan the maze of green hoping for a flicker of movement. His card reads:

English Speaking Guide with Expert Knowledge of Land and Waterbirds in San Blas Area.

The vireo does not budge. Manuel moves upriver.

Roseate spoonbills pass overhead as pink forms with huge flat beaks. I have never seen one before and rise up in the boat, rocking it in my ardor. An osprey sits on a limb, tame as a chicken it seems. Then a kingfisher dives for prey, followed by the sight of a long-necked brown bird, the anhinga, roosting in a tree as the boat slides past. The channel narrows and mangroves press in on us. The shore remains a green wall but it nears, resonating with the cries of dawn. Huge iguanas lumber on the branches and feed off the leaves. They look benign, grotesque, and yet inviting. A great blue heron lifts off and slowly flaps its way across the jungle at San Blas in the state of Nayarit by the vast blue sea. An endless procession of birds sing as the boat drifts into the green heart of the land.

Manuel speaks less and less. He points, stares, his face impassive. He is taking our money but he is living with the birds.

Most Americans do not come here for the wildlife but for the prices. We sip coffee at a café while a man brags to us that he got pesos at the line below San Diego at a helluva of a good exchange and now he and the wife have driven down Baja, ferried over to Nayarit, and are living the life of Riley for next to nothing. Puerto Vallarta, a resort just down the coast, cost too damn much, he snaps. So he has come to San Blas.

When he rolled in last night, he noticed the front tire was bad and now he cannot find the right size in town.

"They'll rob me," he sighs, "they'll do it."

He is convinced of this fact. The face is fleshy, sunburned, and rich with the red hue of stress. He has just talked to another American guy who had been camping out on Matanchen Bay about ten miles south of town. The guy had been sleeping off a good shrimp dinner in his trailer when bam! the door flew open and a Mexican hopped in with a .45. He said he'd like the keys to the 4×4 pronto! you know.

"Well, fellow," the man continues, "he gave over them keys and now he just feels damned glad to be alive."

He stares down at his breakfast and laughs over the incident. Christ, he wonders out loud, how much are they going to clip me for that tire? Brown pelicans cluster on the rocks outside the restaurant as he lets his mind wander into the intricacies of his impending transaction.

Suddenly, he snaps out of his reverie, turns to the fourteen-year-old waitress, and barks, "How about some more coffee, Miss."

Later I ask Manuel about the robbery. He says, sure, they do it. They take the cars, trucks, campers, whatever you have, and cut them up and sell the parts. But not here in town, he says.

"In town," he smiles, "you've got to be good."

Everything can be very good in town. At night, the plaza murmurs, laughs, sings, shouts, chats, smiles, scowls, hollers, hoots, snaps, cheers, snorts, whistles, grunts, sneers, spits, snuffles, yowls, moans, natters, screams, whispers. Drones. At night, the plaza strolls, skips, hops, dances, walks, shuffles, romps, bicycles, runs, and moves to the sigh of the sea. Mostly it waits.

I come to the plaza each night and often during the day. It is dark now, I am standing under a tree bent with the weight of screaming grackles. The woman approaches, skin fresh scrubbed, eyes blue, her clothes all cotton, carefully pure cotton. She says, "I'm from Toronto, how about you?" The lights cast a yellow glow on her skin and hair. She is another rootless one, like myself. She is hunting for something solid, a place where all the fornication, digestion, defecation, and sunrises keep adding up. I do not ask if she has been to Nepal—she probably has. Cleveland? Not likely, but Katmandu, sure. She is looking for a place to be hungry. Once I was doing a story on wetbacks, and I was watching the Border Patrol guy grill a couple of wetbacks in the cell. A few days before it had been 125 degrees in the desert to the south. The men he was questioning were boys, kids fourteen or fifteen, who had just walked forty or fifty miles across that desert in thongs. They were from San Blas in Nayarit. And they did not have to go anywhere to discover hunger. The monument in the center of the square remembers the first revolution of 1810–20. The women strut, the men look. The woman from Toronto walks on.

No one here can doubt for a single second that life is a good thing to have.

One morning we go to the jungle. The bus ride is peasants packed onto benches, boxes tied down on the roof.

We climb off and walk with Manuel down a small village street. The earth is red, the houses faint suggestions of structure. A 7:00 A.M. radio program blares from the coconut log huts as pigs root, dogs bark, and birds relish the dawn hour. Two lilac-crowned parrots sit high in a dead tree on the edge of a clearing. The place is called Singaita.

The parrots are players in a dying world. Men catch them and sell them to tourists. Most of such birds die, especially the adults who cannot seem to learn to love the cage. I ask Manuel if there is a good bird guide in Spanish and he rocks with laughter.

"There are no Mexican birders," he replies.

The jungle is going away, the parrots are disappearing, the crocodiles have about been shot out. Twenty-five years ago, the river teemed with crocs, men would go out and kill twenty or thirty in a night. Manuel has not seen one in several years. When men now hear of a crocodile, they take their guns and go out and stay out until they kill it. The iguanas are slaughtered also, stuffed, and sold to tourists. The jaguar is seldom seen and then killed on sight. Plantations take more and more of the jungle each year.

I look up and see a coppery tailed trogon feeding near a papaya grove. A russet-crowned motmot calls from a tree. The birds blaze with color. A painted bunting—red breast, blue head—sits on a branch like an Easter egg. Manuel follows a red earth trail under palms, mangroves, mahogany, Mexican cedar, strangler fig. A squirrel cuckoo yowls in the bush and half-wild cattle crash ahead into the *marisma*, a savannah.

A laughing falcon calls from deep in the forest. Manuel says they shoot the hawks and falcons too. They shoot everything. But, he allows, bullets are getting harder to obtain.

"To protect the wildlife?"

"No," he snaps, "to protect themselves. They are afraid of the revolution."

The laughing falcon goes hah, hah, hah. The book says it can laugh up to fourteen times.

Most of the time gnats are in the air, not revolution. Dusk is falling, and we walk near a small landing field just north of town. Two women, their dresses shining with green and red and blue, talk and hold babies on their hips as children at the nearby fishing school go through a military drill. As the women stroll, they slap their legs and arms and faces, their necks and backs. Their words never skip a beat. They move through chickens scratching in the dirt, amiable spastics enjoying a San Blas sunset.

I drink often at the hotel and one day meet a man who collects anecdotes of the violence waiting beneath the calm. He edits the English-language paper in Guadalajara and is here to comp meals and rooms at the hotel in exchange for a glowing story. The woman with him is good-looking and buxom. They are both old surfers, veterans of the sixties, a time the perfect waves attracted bronzed bodies to San Blas, survivors of an era when people then drifted into perfect drug deals. He is more solid now, he tells me, he has his staff, his product, his niche in Mexican society. He is a student of his new home, a *Yanqui* rooted south of line.

There are villages in Jalisco, he explains, where there are no men who can work, they have all gone to *El Norte* for seasonal labor. You go these places and you find old men, women, small children. Everyone waits for the return of the men and the sudden injection of cash. The authorities maintain control, he purrs, by simple means. Sometimes they shoot a man who is rising among the peasants, sometimes they kill a promising leader in the labor movement. For years he has been running his newspaper and he is full of stories he can never write.

There was, he smiles, this rising young bureaucrat in one department who complained about the level of graft on a government contract. Suddenly he found himself frozen out of the paper flow. He hastened to Mexico City and sought out his friends, his patrons in high places. But they would no longer see him. His phone sat silent on the table in his hotel room.

So he went to a cabin in the nearby mountains with his staff and mistress. The newspapers said it was a faulty valve on the kerosene heater. The editor laughs. Apparently, the gas valve shot the bureaucrat in the back of the head.

The woman was spared. She was sent out so that the right people back home would know what had happened. And mark the lesson well.

San Blas? God, he loves San Blas, been coming here faithfully since 1964. But the town is empty now, he sighs. The hotels have no guests, the real season will begin in a month with the advent of winter. The crazy state of the economy has caused some cancellations, and a spate of killings has not helped either. In the past year or two, fifteen Americans have been murdered on Highway 15, he continues, the main road down Mexico's west coast. A colonel who had retired to San Blas was gunned down near Culiacán. And three in San Blas itself; there have been some hard moments. Two Americans made mistakes. The girl they found buried on the beach. The boy was tied to a rock below the high-tide mark. Something about drugs, he thinks.

"Bad for business," he says.

The country always seems so placid, the colors so bright. The anger can slip right past you for a while. I was in an Indian village below Orizaba once, the typical visitor acclimating to 10,000 feet before slapping on the crampons and hacking my way up the peak's glacier. There was nothing to eat but chicken and beans. A pig would wander in and out of the town's general store. On the edge of the village slumbered the remains of the old hacienda. Big stone walls, the fine mansion in the center for the owner, well-made granaries, huge stables for the horses. I walked

into the courtyard where two guys worked on a broken-
down car, a radio blaring. Nearby chickens scratched
where there had once been formal gardens. Peasants had
moved into the various rooms, the place was now a tenement. I wheeled and looked back at the wall. Gaping holes
marked where cannons had punctured it in the revolution
between 1910 and 1920. In those years, one out of every
eight Mexicans died violently. There is this thing sleeping
beneath the calm of Mexico, a black, hard thing.

You can see it writhing and breathing in the photographs of the revolution, the men dangling like ornaments
from trees in Morelos, the dead staring at the blue sky over
Chihuahua, the soldiers without shoes facing the camera
with Indian eyes as boxcars drag them from the villages to
the machine guns of the twentieth century, the children
with bandoliers of bullets standing shorter than their
guns, the women moving with the armies like dark summer storms across the land. Over drinks everyone can remember kin who faced a firing squad and lived or faced a
firing squad and died and sometimes I think every old
adobe wall in the country has stories to tell if only we had
the energy to pry the bullets loose from their sleeping
places in the tired, baked mud. For Americans, the whole
country is at times Wallace Beery grinning from the
screen as Pancho Villa. I can remember as a child seeing
this face laughing on a twelve-inch black and white
screen. But in Mexico, the candy is shaped like a human
skull. If you paste Nacho's jailhouse photographs on the
wall and look into the face, you will catch a glimpse of it.
Black, for sure, and I sense very hard.

After a week or so in San Blas, the local cookery makes
its inroads on my digestive system and I become at times a
prisoner of my hotel room. I read Russian novels about
the meaninglessness of life and the vitality of serfs. I spend
hours on the balcony outside the room staring down at
pages and drinking. Mike and Marta leave and a gray-

haired guy takes the room next door. He likes to fish, speaks Spanish, and is always busy with his line and tackle, or out about the town on various errands. Everyone knows him, he has come here for years. We nod, and that is it.

Late one afternoon I sit and watch the sea. Nothing happens out there but low waves and frigate birds riding high in the sky. The man comes out of his room, pulls over a chair, and sits down with a liter of tequila. Yes, certainly, I say.

A few years ago, the doctors took his lung. Cancer. A year ago, he had a quadruple bypass. He is lean, the kind of man who has been skinny every day of his life. He tilts back on his chair and as he talks, looks straight out to sea. God, he loves to fish, each day he goes off with a local Mexican boy and drags in tuna and bass. He's been coming here for seven years. He says, "I hate big towns."

He went into the Army in 1939. The judge said, kid, it's either the Army or jail. He stayed thirty years in the military. He was a tough kid so he went into the paratroopers. A grunt, he fought three wars and has no complaint on that score.

My hair is long, I have not shaven, and my wars are written on my face. I say, "Look, I was in the streets during Nam hold placards." He nods. It never matters. The conversation is always the same, something about how the war was fucked or fucked over or ruined by politicians or something. We pour another drink.

Now he carries a packet of nitro capsules in his pocket and when he moves he takes them.

The day is sliding fast toward sunset and he sits facing west with the light flooding his face. It is a pinched face, with small eyes, narrow features. His right biceps sports a tattoo, the image ripples as he cocks his arm and throws down shot after shot of tequila. The Army, he says, sent him to language school and then on to Quito, Ecuador, to create that nation's paratroops. Jesus, he loved Ecuador.

The Marine guards there at the embassy went nuts, every upper-class senorita in the capital saw them a ticket out to the land of rich Americans. He found that a former president had been an ardent fisherman and had a lake at 13,-000 feet stocked with trout. There was nothing up there but Indians and they knew nothing about fishing. When the president left office, the trout were forgotten and grew to monstrous size. The paratrooper heard about this fishery and had the Navy wing him in and drop a small boat to boot.

He tosses down another shot as he remembers those big trout. The rains never stop in the mountains and he fished in cold showers. The Indians would clean the fish and take the heads and guts. They made a soup. Soon he had them build him a hut so that he could get out of the rain. Ecuador, what fishing.

He is rolling now. He comes down to San Blas several times a year because it is not the United States. The tequila flows, the gnats rise up for their night feeding, and he talks on. He has seen a lot of places. He can live like the natives and he has. He has been defending America's borders for his entire life by violating them, by reaching out to other places. But still, he likes borders. He was sitting in his house in the States watching cable television one night when this ad comes on advertising a hotel for sale, a real nice place by the sea, and suddenly he realized it was this very hotel, the one where we're slopping down tequila in San Blas. And this fact outraged him, one of his borders had been stormed.

His life ended in Nam. The sky is turning red now and the battles of Southeast Asia rumble across the veranda. He was around My Lai, he saw things happen. He had to testify at the congressional hearings. He saw drugs eat into his army, saw the ranks split by race. He is bitter about these matters.

The press, he spits, the press ruined the war. They put the Army on television but they didn't put Charley on. He pours another shot. He is a small man but very hard and well disciplined. He can get it done, anything you name, he can get it done. In Nam this major said to him, Christ, if the things we're doing get in the papers we'll go to Leavenworth. They would cut the ears off Charley and pin them to the chest with a bayonet and leave a printed calling card. Fuck the liberals, this was war. It spills out. He is not apologizing, he is simply talking. His heart is shot, one lung gone, and now he is dictating the war to a peace marcher from the sixties. We are both loaded.

Suddenly, the voice alters, grows softer, the pace of the words slows. Six months ago, he almost whispers, his daughter died, killed herself. She told him, you can only marry once and if you do and it doesn't work out, that was it. It didn't work out and she fell apart. She saw doctors, tried to take her life a few times.

The sea birds have gone to ground in front of the hotel, the slap of small waves and swish of palm fronds washes the air. He takes another shot. His speech remains unimpaired, the alcohol cannot touch his wound.

She would call him at night, he says, and they would talk. She was in the Midwest, he was on the coast, the calls would come late at night and the talk would go on and on. She tried living with a guy, had a baby. Nothing seemed to help. He'd hop on a plane, fly out there all the time, he felt like a yo-yo. One night the phone rang and she said she'd had enough, she couldn't live with anyone and she couldn't live alone. He said, hey, don't talk that way, come out here, come out here and we'll fix it, we'll put something together. He went on and on and talked her down. She said, okay, I'll be out in a week.

He got the next call at 1:30 A.M. and a detective asked if he was so-and-so and was so-and-so his daughter. Yeah, he said. Well, she's dead, the voice replied, and you'd better call the coroner in thirty minutes.

He'd always planned to be buried in Arlington along

with all the rest of the guys. Now he's going to being buried in the plot right next to her. The tequila is doing no good now, the memories keep coming. The man says he has thought about that night a thousand times, a thousand times. The sun is sinking into the sea. Bats flash across a blood red sky.

People march down the streets of San Blas on November 20 as the town celebrates the beginning of the 1910 Revolution. San Blas is drugged with history—in 1810, another revolution visited, the town priest jumped off a cliff and became a legend. Today there is music and food, the sun glows with promise. All over Mexico it is a big holiday. Francisco Madero said in 1910, "I have designated Sunday, the 20th day of November, for all the towns in the republic to rise in arms after 6 o'clock P.M." He tossed out this suggestion from the safety of El Paso. The Mexicans rose up, the regime slaughtered them, and ever since local folks have been celebrating the hell out of the occasion.

We take a cab to Tepic and the same festive air floods the city's railroad station. On a television by the taco stand, the president, El Señor, reviews a parade in Mexico City's Zócalo. He raises his arms over his head to the cheers of the crowd. And then he walks like a king between two columns of supporters who bow to him and reach out to brush their fingers against his sleeve.

It is a revolutionary day. I will never know Mexico. It is beyond my range.

NACHO

I want out now. Fear is not the right word. The feeling is more compelling than fear. I tell Art we will learn no more, so let's go. He argues. We go to a cheap café near the fence. He thinks we will find more. I know he is right. Three *cholos* from Buenos Aires sit at a nearby table, their arms dancing with tattoos, the faces a mask. One wears thick black leather bands around his wrists, gleaming studs rising from the dark hide. I think: it is not the fists that are warning me, it is not the guns dangling from the cops hands, it is not whiff of muscle coming off the ring of the word "commandante." It is the mirror. I am looking into some kind of mirror and if I stay right now I will see something I do not want to see. It is just time.

She sits in her garden, the Sunday light pouring over her like love. Her hair is very long but this morning it is tied up around her head. The body is all curves, quite hard. She works like a man. There are two coffee cups, she has just ground the beans, brewed the pot, and the scent is wonderful mingling with the smell of mani-cured soil around her flower beds. An unfinished crossword puzzle looks up from the ground.

She is weeping. This is tacky, she says, I can't go on. I listen. This is my task in this place. The house is spotless, organized. There is no television, walls of books keep watch, two excellent speakers purr with music, blues, folk, rock. A candle burns, always. A flame keeping the faith with life.

In the garden it is simpler. Sunshine, rich fat rays fall on my skin and my cells feed like starved rats on the bounty. I look into her face and know I have failed again. There are all the same words, the same understandings, the fact that no one wants to own anyone, no one wants to be a burden, no one wants to make life any harder or more bizarre than it seems to spin along anyway. Her hands are very rough from building things, fixing things. Nearby her big motorcycle rests. She can do anything she can think of, she is very competent. I envy her such command over objects and situations.

"What are you doing with your life?" she asks.

"I improvise."

How does she stay so clean, I wonder. How many hours a day does it take to maintain this cell of sanity and decency. I envy her her rack of coffee cups in the kitchen, I envy her the plants in pots all so healthy. I envy her.

I wait, let the torrents of words pour out. The tears make her eyes glisten in the wonderful light.

"What do you really want?" I finally ask.

"I want to be happy in my work, to do something worthwhile, to be loved and to give love."

I would too.

> *A hero doesn't have too many emotions. He's got to be above all that, you see. Leave that to the women. Let them be tearful and sensitive and gentle. The hero is gentle, of course, with the weak, and strong with the bad.*
> *—Charles Bronson, 1986*

Art combs Tucson and digs up old dealers, young dealers, a gaggle of *cholos* trying to deal with a brave, new drug world. The raw facts are elegant in their simplicity. Nogales, Sonora, has grown from 25,000 souls to 200,000 in a few decades. By 1984, Americans drop $123 million a day buying drugs, says one study. The flow of narcotics north from Latin America has shifted in part from Florida to Arizona. Some of this spare change flows through the *colonias* of the border town.

There is this old dealer on the south side of Tucson, a man the police say has been involved in at least seventy drug-related killings in the metropolitan area. He says he is weary of the game now.

"I know everyone," he says, "from the highest to the lowest dealers, not only in Tucson but in the United States and Mexico. I've kept records almost from the start when I was first getting busted and I kept track of everything. Now everyone on the goddamn south side is dealer, when the season starts in October they're like a bunch of damned ants at a picnic. Then you see them all buying new pickups, building higher patio walls, and trying to build a bigger house than the other dealers. The trouble is you can't trust the bastards, if they don't kill you, they snitch you off to the cops. Then there's the cops, there's a million damn cops out there now, they fall all over themselves. That's why I don't do business anymore. It's too damn dangerous."

The young dealer sings a similar song with a different melody line.

"In the sixties," he says, "you could trust people. The cops were honest, the addicts were honest, and you didn't have to worry about getting killed for your drugs. We knew who the cops were and you took your chances when you sold stuff but not like today. Now you can't trust anyone. There's cops all over the place. In the seventies, the killings started, a lot of Cubans came here and more and more Mexicans from Nogales moved here and started selling dope. Then they started killing each other and ripping off people. Still even then most of the stuff was controlled by home boys. Then in the late seventies the big-time *cholos* moved in from Nogales and cocaine became real popular. That's the trouble, all those guys from the other side control everything, the home boys can't keep up with them. You have to buy almost everything from them now."

The cop, the mentor in the café with his sure, superior ways, says simply, "The drug scene has changed a lot from the seventies, the big change coming around '78 or '79. The old deal would go something like this: you go down and say you want to buy a thousand pounds and the guy would say fifty percent now and give me the rest a week later. So you take the load and then, hey, you get busted and lose it all. So you go back and he says, okay, I'll charge you more for the next load and you pay me with the profits from it. Now you go down there and say you want a thousand pounds and you get it and you get busted and lose and you go back and say, hey, I lost it. And they say, pay us now. And if you don't they kill you."

It's not just the cars, the stereos and VCRs that have slipped from our economic grasp. The old American can-do has met a fiercer drive. I smile at the thought.

Art is down in Nogales chasing details. He sits in the plaza right by the gate, a big monstrosity of flowing cement, flowers, and benches. There are people everywhere, laughing, talking, selling, buying. The air smells of all the human hungers. The women are so clean, they walk out of huts and shacks, flies swarming around their faces, and yet the clothes scream with cleanliness and their skin looks soft and scrubbed. And now they are walking in the plaza, the hips jutting as they sway on their high heels.

Suddenly a dozen Federales ride into the plaza on horseback, carbines at ready across the saddles. The horses seem to stomp on the pavement, sweat glows from their hides, power flexes in their thighs. The twentieth century is winding down, the machine gun has replaced the six-shooter, but the horse breaks out of the cobwebs of history, stomps in the plaza and still matters, and still says power. They circle once, then tie up their horses. Art is spellbound by the sight. Then he notices he is all alone. Everyone has vanished. The birds in the trees fall still, or so it seems to him. He tells me this later, excitedly. He does not say what it means. It is, of course, something he already knew.

But now he feels it.

Lupita chews delicately. She says, "He couldn't talk to his aunt about what he did because she was afraid of him. He couldn't talk to his mother because he didn't want her to suffer anymore. The killings? They hurted him but he said he had to do it."

> *... items of high civilization, as it exists in other countries, which are absent from the texture of American life. ... No sovereign, no court, no personal loyalty, no aristocracy, no church, no clergy, no army, no diplomatic service, no country gentlemen, no palaces, no castles, nor manors, nor old country-houses, nor parsonages, nor thatched cottages, nor ivied ruins; no cathedrals, nor abbeys, nor Norman churches; no great Universities, nor public schools—no Oxford, nor Eton, nor Harrow; no literature, no novels, no museums, no pictures, no political society, no sporting class—no Epsom nor Ascot!*
> *—Henry James, 1878*

The woman drives. Her shoes are on now, the sunroof rolled back, black air pouring down on us. We stop at the store for cigarettes, the music flaming from the radio, words, my God, the words, long words, hard words, transportation, density, comprehensive plan, government, words all good and true and false, sounds empty of everything but the force that lurks behind them, I hear the guitar but the rhythms are slipping in the clouds of smoke, the hand switches to a sitar and the pick moves with strange flicks now. I look over at the woman, she is wearing glasses now, the words sound so serious. But the eyes burn. It is time we did something, she says, we grew up here, we have come of age, it is time we acted. Time, she notes, is running out.

I stare at the rap sheet typed by the Mexican clerk. It states: "12/20/73. Ignacio Robles Valencia. Convicted of murder. Sent to Prison."
He has just turned fourteen.

The meeting is full in the Unitarian Church. We sit in back, the coffee urn nearby, I sip bitter brew from the styrofoam cup. She is very alert here, these are her people, she knows them all, the voice purrs in my ear naming the players. The panel facing the audience runs from environmentalist through developers, the typical Sunbelt United Nations delegation of needs and anger. The issue is called the buffer, a slab of land surrounding various wild parks abutting the city, a *cordon sanitaire* that will be free of high-density buildings, kept free of the millions beating against the gates of older ways of life.
The faces are quite content, the skin white and unblemished. I feel sanity crushing my body—"riparian habitat, creatures, wildlife corridors, housing"—my frame buckles, the coffee does not help, the eyes of the panel see straight into the future and they tell me it is all absolutely a straight line with no tickets for speeding and no accidents. If we will only listen and act rationally.
She says, "Had enough?"
I say, "Yes."

But I have never had enough of anything.

I walk out the door, phrases pinging against my ears— "Quality of life, open space, amenities."

I stare at the rap sheet, neatly typed key by key by the Mexican clerk. The line states: "11/24/74. Ignacio Robles Valencia (A) El Nacho Robles: arrested for robbery and violence. Sent to Prison."

He will be fifteen in a week or two.

The car is perfect, seats perfect, paint perfect, engine, shift, buttons, power. Perfect. We flow into the traffic, strands of light slicing the night. She drives well, the shifts smooth, the lane changes a statement of self. The tach sweeps upward. I eye the red line, my foot stays still, my head wants to slam the accelerator to the floor.

We are talking transportation but we both love the traffic. The city at night seethes, there are the electric fires, the anxious faces of the other drivers as they hunt houses, bars, malls, corners, lanes for a warm hand and wet fantasy. The city is bicultural, she says, it is a rich thing to keep and preserve. I eye the tach. We are going nowhere but I want it to be fast.

We pull over at a hotel, walk toward the bar. The marble and wood inside beckons. She stops and says, "Let's get out of here."

The car snaps awake, the lights flip up.

Lupita is puzzled by the question about cars. Her brows briefly knit, then a faint shrug passes through her.

"No, he didn't have a car. He would borrow one when he needed one—you had to be careful if you loaned him a car because if he got stopped with the merchandise, he would jump out and run away and then you would lose your car. When he came up from Mexico, he jumped through the fence and walked for two or three days."

We stream northward into the foothills. She speaks of some land she owns, acres of pure desert on the edge of town. To go there, walk, listen, the peace. She plans to build a house, the perfect house, but will she? The land is perfect now, you know. I see her face in the glow of the dashboard. She is looking straight ahead speaking into the safety glass.

"It doesn't matter," I say.

Lupita speaks easily now. It does not matter what we want or what we will do with it.

"When he was thirteen," she says, "he did his first assassination. She was an old lady, he told me, real old, and she was just walking down the street—'just passing through,' he said—and he jumped her. He wanted some money. He killed her with a screwdriver. He got thirteen cents.

"He went to prison on that island, Islas Tres Marias, the place in the Gulf of California called the Islands of the Assassins. He escaped from there. How? I don't know. Once he escaped from prison by the *ley fuga* or law of flight—there were fifty-eight men offered the chance to run. This was in 1980 or 1981. Nacho took off, the guards fired, he was one of fifteen survivors. The other time was in the Nogales prison. He was sick, he had those things in his arm, those needles and tubes, he pulled them out and then killed the guard and left."

> *[They] are not pleased with some of them [the rules], in particular with those which bind them to strike root in the land; for all, or most, of them intend to deal with these lands as they did with the Islands first populated, namely, to exhaust them, to destroy them, then to leave them.*
> *—Hernán Cortés on his conquistadores*

The hotel hides against the mountain, I expect a coyote to walk across the beams of the headlights. There is an unsaid thing inside the machine and we leave it unsaid. The saguaros and mesquite brood by the roadside and then the parking lot appears and the attendants wait by the door for trade. I direct her to a side lot. She says, "I usually have it parked." This will not do, I can't say why, so we walk back to the hotel.

Inside the lobby a large geode with purple crystals is on display like a ripe fruit broken open for a beach party in the tropics. The carpet is silent and spreads under my feet with a faint echo of a Navajo pattern. There is a conspiracy here of quiet good taste and all the sounds are soft and all the voices muted.

We go to the bar. The grand piano sits dead at the moment, the small tables surrounded by bands of cushioned chairs. Large windows to the north reach up two floors and through the glass the mountain snores in the darkness. The blue eye of a pool, carefully sized so as not to suggest swim meets and grisly work-outs, peers up from the ground just past our table.

I am rooted to a city where things happen fast enough that within five years time everyone can feel old, share the sensation of those ancients in other regions who lean back on a chair in front of the general store and remark about the changes on Main Street, the vanished buildings, ground, folkways. I remember when this ground was desert, the holdings of a nearby ranch. I came out for a party, listened to the birds in the trees, strolled down to the corral, and threw a blond woman up on a 2,500-pound Belgian horse named Max and watched the indifference in the animal's eye and caught the scent of excitement coming off the woman. Steps led up from the stables, wide, stone steps suggesting a garden centuries old in some English estate, and the city seemed very far away. Now the hotel sits here, with its golf course, townhouses, disco, and assorted delights. I can remember when the ground was pretty much the way it had been the day Cortés burned

his ships and left his men on the beach to win Mexico
or die. Which is to say, I can remember back four or five
years.

We sit and order drinks. Talk is pleasant. What is to be
done about the town? There is a bit of local language
here—in this city everything that grieves and spooks people is an act of the city, everything that holds and woos
people is a feature of the town. Her words make a lot of
sense in the same way that logic always does: they sound
right. I have no argument, except rejoinders for the sake of
argument. I lack the facility to think. So I spar.

I look at the other tables and everywhere I see the
threads and gestures of wealth. I think, these are Nacho's
people but they have yet to meet him and his friends. Just
as gourmets often fail to press the flesh with wheat farmers in the Dakotas or with bakers busy feeding the ovens at
3:00 A.M. I touch her hand. Outside the window, against
the rockface of the mountain, an artificial waterfall tumbles down a cliff into the caress of an electric lamp that
fires a glow into the spray.

My mind is a blank. I know the woman would argue this
point, note carefully her statements and my replies, but it
is so: my mind is a blank. I hear Bob Dylan in my head
singing:

> I dreamed I saw St. Augustine,
> Alive with fiery breath.
> And I dreamed I was amongst the ones
> That put him out to death.
> Oh, I awoke in anger,
> So alone and terrified,
> I put my fingers against the glass
> And bowed my head and cried.

I look into her eyes, quick with intelligence. We are
drifting past business, beyond the tasks of good govern-

ment, sound organizing, guidelines, task forces, commis-
sions, study groups, newsletters, blueprints, comprehensive plans, designs for living. I hear Dylan's thin, frail
voice. He is back from his motorcycle accident, he has
been gone for what—eighteen months? two years?—a
vanished man since "Blonde on Blonde," and I am lying
on the floor of a cheap apartment in the Bay Area with
my belly full of Zinfandel, perhaps the only American
wine that is unique, certainly the only American wine pio-
neered by a Hungarian who was eaten by crocodiles in
Panama, and I am lying there listening to a radio station
and they begin to play the new album, "John Wesley
Harding," and I look at the dirty walls, think of the novel
waiting in the typewriter in the next room, and then stop
thinking and listen as the voice, a voice now thin and
frail, the snarl at bay for the moment, a voice that decides to speak of mysteries and, Boom! St. Augustine
comes out of the speakers, the man of the City of God,
and he is alive as you or I. The empire, the fucking empire, Jack, well, it's going now, not to worry, the pump
doesn't work either 'cause the Vandals stole the handle
but we've known that since "Highway 61 Revisited," and
the damn voice is a needle, a kind of hatpin, stuck right
in my head, and I look over at the woman with her smile
and bright eyes and I'm gone, shit, I'm gone, left, vanished, hit the road. An old man I once knew told
me when I asked what people did for a living in a Mexican
border town, "Well, they eat each other's bones," and he
booms into my head now and temporarily blurs out
Dylan and the woman weaves in and out—we are talking
about the Holocaust and I can hear myself saying
things—but St. Augustine has me by the throat, I am sure
he knew Nacho, maybe Nachito was his dealer dropping
by the abbey from time to time with a gram or two, or
perhaps they met in the streets and Nacho walked up and
said, "Good morning," and asked which fork in the road

led to the Holy City, said he was tired of Nogales and the damn work and gunfire and hey, I think I'm outta here, you know, and St. Augustine, he purred with that fiery breath and Nacho fell into a dream about death and putting people to death, a screwdriver flashing in his hand. I reach out and feel her fingers on the tabletop, and we have forgotten about parkways versus freeways. Her mind is so quick, I delight in the ping pong of our words and then I am gone again and I lack the courage to tell her where, I know better than to admit to such things. The Bishop of Hippo, Augie himself speaks up, it is four hundred years since Christ got nailed and St. Augustine waits on the coast of North Africa for history to unwind because that is the key, he believes in history, in this following that following something else, and if he could look inside my head he'd exorcise it, call for a general house cleaning because he is finished with the mysteries, with these one-time mystic shots in the dark. And I have barely begun with them. Christ, I think, maybe Augie would have some compassion if he'd ever seen a comprehensive plan or listened to speakers outline salvation as a matter of units per acre, open space, and solar water heaters. Dammit, he once knew better, he once confessed he wanted to be saved but not yet! No, not yet, Lord. He is sitting there in North Africa, the civilized world failing before his eyes, and now he is denouncing woman, the nasty, juicy wenches, the core of all the Earth Goddesses that have the forest folk and desert folk doing hellish dances into the dark hours, the hydra-headed female that beckons, calls, whispers about the mysteries in the trees, the wonders to be felt in the *despoblados*, the black rites under a moon as full as a breast. The bitch teeming with disorder and fertility and possibility.

I try to snap back, try to leave the landscape of North Africa, a place I have never seen but am absolutely sure of. There is a bowl of nuts on the table in this cocktail lounge and my hand reaches forward and I grab some and put them in my mouth and carefully chew. Order. The woman comes back into focus, I finger the fabric of her coat, look about me and see the quiet conversations, cherish the carefully muted carpet, swallow my red wine. There is no way to talk about the fact that sometime after the birth of Christ a thing called history dethroned a thing called mystery and took over a thing called our civilization and made it orderly, here and now, and capable of being finished, of being finite, organized, an assembly line for human souls. And that I want out. I have tried that conversation, I have tried to explain the drift. I always fail. I lack the capacity. I want to say that comprehensive plans matter but don't really matter because I don't know what matters but I sense what does not. That is why I am rubbing the fabric of your coat right now, that is the exact reason, see? No? Well, I can't say any more than that. This has been happening every day of my life. I love the red line, it does not happen there. I know from what I am told that revelations come from quiet places, but I am sixteen centuries after the Bishop of Hippo and the quiet places have moved, the speed increased in the rush toward solitude.

I finish my wine. We get up.

I am hungry for the records, the safety of the printed word where all of Nacho's deeds are spelled out in detail. Art and I drive back to the line and visit the police station again. The request seems simple.

Of course, it is impossible. The aide tells us we must speak to the lieutenant. The lieutenant explains that federal law and the citizen's right of confidentiality forbids the copying of police records—"muy difficile"—and there is nothing that can be done, so sorry. He wears a brown shirt, sits in a windowless room, and stares out at us with a face like a plate of cold food. Perhaps, if we go to the Palace of Justice. . . . I wait, my ear ready for the clue—Is there no way out of this difficulty, Señor? No solution that will work for both of us?—the words are ignored, the money stays in my pocket.

The marble stairs of the Palace of Justice climb up facing windows of red and yellow, empty Coke bottles lined up in squads on the landings. The building hums with people, women with babies, lawyers, tattooed punks with handcuffs gleaming on their wrists who dutifully follow cops. The sound of typewriters saturates the air and every door has a line of supplicants. We discover the commandante in a hall, walkie-talkie in hand. He is in his thirties, it is 10:00 A.M. and he is ripped, vapors of booze billowing off him. He has been in Nogales four months and can be of no service. The magistrate has a very clean desk, a class ring (University of Sonora, Nogales branch), and presents certain difficulties. The documents of El Nacho (yes, I know of him, I worked on one prosecution) can only be transmitted to another police agency. Yes, of course he is dead now, but the law . . . however, perhaps, there is a way. We could copy certain sections—there will be a fee—come back next Wednesday.

His room is spotless, a few law books leaning against each other in a bookcase and at the far end a second desk where his secretary sits and studies her nails. She is in her twenties, the skirt is quite tight, and her main task seems to be leaving and entering the room so we can study her form.

The young judge is very friendly. *Ley fuga?* Ah yes, he tells us, you will never find it written in any law book but nevertheless it is a law. Nacho, oh, I tried him myself, and I know he survived a *ley fuga* here in the Nogales prison and I have heard he survived one at Islas Tres Marias.

We explain Nacho's system for distributing drugs in the United States and the magistrate listens attentively.

Nacho, we say, had a distributor in Tucson—*"claro,"* the judge smiles. And he had a distributor in Phoenix—*"perfecto,"* he beams.

We return a few days later for more talk and then, as if by magic, huge files come rumbling out of nowhere. The case records. We cross the street to a copying center, drop a wheelbarrowful of pesos, and it is done. The long documents in obscure Spanish take us back to the acts.

I am sitting in my office late at night. The piece of paper is almost a decade old. It talks. Robbery with violence. Two Americans go to Nogales to buy marijuana from Nacho. They argue over the price and one of the Americans picks up a rock. Nacho whips out a switchblade and says, "Give me all the money, you mother." His friend, El Chato, grabs one American by the throat while Nacho empties his pocket. They take his watch and a hundred dollars.

Or three armed men point guns at the guards in the Nogales prison. It is 9:30 A.M., October 30, 1977, and Nacho is one of the armed men. A guard moves to shut the main gate, and Nacho waves his gun and says, "Okay, you whores and bastards, we're going out now." He grabs a guard, puts a gun to his head, and moves forward. Nacho and his friends—El Teco, El Chicago, and others—rush outside. A red pickup and a brick-colored car with tinted windows pull up and the people in the vehicles pass out guns. A guard reaches for the door of the car, Nacho puts a gun to his throat. A firefight ensues. Some men leave in the cars, some race to a nearby bus. Others disappear into the city.

> *Is not the tremendous strength in men of the impulse to creative work in every field precisely due to the feeling of playing a relatively small part in the creation of new living beings, which con-*

*stantly impels them to an over-compensation in
achievement?*

—*Karen Horney*

We do not go to the car. The desert beckons out the huge
windows of the hotel. A paved path winds beside an artificial stream and well-placed lights highlight the mesquite,
palo verde, and saguaros that dot the slope. We are talking
easily now, her body is pressed against mine as we walk.
The night air is cool but not cold, the liquor gives us a soft
glow of warmth.

In my office, a file drawer bulges with court records. I
keep reading them in my weak Spanish, savoring the
small angry boy hidden behind the docket numbers and
sentences. I think of the knife, the screwdriver, sometimes, it is said, the scissors. The first contact, then the
plunge, the blade coursing through the flesh until arrested
in its adventure by the hilt or the hand. He could always
feels his victim's breath on his face as he killed. There is
nothing in the records of how this breath, this hot, gasping
air, felt flowing across his face.

I remember my breakfast with Lupita. She shrugged at
his prison time. So? She said, "He figured he would wind
up back in prison, he was used to it. He'd lived there since
he was thirteen. Inside, he had people afraid of him and he
would make them work for him and bring him food, cigarettes, women. I visited him once in the Nogales prison
along with his woman. He was in isolation for killing a
guard but we just walked right in. His room was clean and
he was clean. He had a bathroom, bed, kitchen wall, it was
roomy. Here he was in isolation but he could take a
woman to bed."

The path is not smooth and we almost stumble at times
and then we hit a line of steps and go up and up and come
to a deep pool of water with cascades from above booming
into it. I stare down and can see fish. The water is pumped

uphill and then falls downhill, day and night, summer or winter. It is a special effect.

We climb up another set of steps to a kind of terrace. The city lights can be glimpsed from here. She pulls off her panties and we make love as the column of water falls to earth, again and again.

He has been arrested, imprisoned, threatened. Oscar Monroy Rivera is fifty-four, fat, short, and wears a light blue tank top, shorts, and sandals. He does not speak, he announces, the finger jabbing forward, the brow furrowed, and every few moments he leaps from his chair in the book-lined study, wheels around, and paces the long narrow room. But he never stops talking. This is the Bahia del Silencio, the bay of silence; a long, hand-carved wooden sign outside proclaims this fact to the world. Monroy is a Mexican intellectual, the house is his mental prison, the silence—elusive when one is within range of his booming voice—is outside his home, the denial by his government of his existence, of his words, of his passion.

He pigeonholes Nacho quickly, "another poor devil, a victim of the society." The Nachos are not the important thing, he says, look for the big operators, the government, the rich Americans, the whole life of the frontier drenched with drugs, money, and death. Monroy almost begs to be dismissed as a closet scholar, a windbag. He has written forty books, plus nine hundred articles. He smiles and says he is the most prolific Sonoran of this century. On his typewriter he has glued the sentence that states that words must be written with blood or they are nothing. He seems to be an actor giving a performance in this long room tucked away on a side street near the railroad tracks.

But he is not to be dismissed. His life is intermeshed with the life of his city, and with the flowering of the

traffic. He has been imprisoned several times for protest-
ing corruption and naming names in the local drug industry. Twice contracts have been put out on his life.
But he is not so easy to kill. Because he is rooted
here.

He was born right on the fence in the building that now
houses Restaurant Elvira—still a family business. As a
child, he and his friends would use slingshots to knock out
street lights in the United States; sometimes American
kids would return fire with .22s. Once, when a department
store in Nogales, Arizona, partially burned, he and some
friends looted it and passed the hot goods to pals over the
fence. He attended the Mexican public schools and hated
them, dreaming of one day winning the lottery, buying a
plane, and bombing the building. His father disappeared
and his mother (who died of cancer at age forty-eight)
raised the nine children. For Nogales, they were middle
class.

Monroy escaped to Mexico City in the mid-fifties, entered the university, and flourished as an intellectual. He
can be seen in old photos with his wife and child, or standing up in a suit at poetry readings. He returned to Nogales
in 1970 in the hope, he says, of bringing some culture to
the remembered wasteland of his youth and of entering
the politics of the state. A stream of books resulted, one, *El
Profeta del silencio* (*The Prophet of Silence*, 1972), was a
success nationwide and went through several editions. It
concerned El Bulla, a local beggar who finally died at age
seventy-four, a man diseased and almost mute. Monroy
used him as a device for criticizing the corruption and
cruelty of life in Nogales. He also, in 1974, wrote the pref-
ace to *A Visit to the Prison*, an anonymous account of life
in the Nogales pen. The little book says things like this: "A
very frank and gratified smile crowned the lips of el señor
licenciado Restres, director of the prison, who in those
moments felt profoundly grateful to the personages of the

political state to who he owed his position . . . which allowed him to receive honors . . . from the distinguished prisoners who offered him money, feasts, honors. . . . In the meantime the lawyer Everardo Jimeno was conversing . . . about the knowledge and the art with which he is able to take drug traffickers out of jail in just hours. . . . With fifty or one hundred thousand pesos it is just a matter of hours."

There is a section of *A Visit to the Prison* that describes an escape by some of the inmates, their recapture, and what happened to them back in their cells. First, the clothes were removed, then the brass knuckles were used. One man falls on his knees and says, "By your sainted mother, don't torture me. No more! I will tell you anything you want, everything." He urinates and defecates on himself.

They pick him up, his hair is grabbed and pulled, they carry him across the room. And sit him down on the electric hotplate. The stove hisses, the smell of burnt flesh wafts across the room. He struggles to rise, but two soldiers hold him down.

A second man is put on the stove and eventually faints. The next day they return for him, carrying a hammer. The man has opened his veins with his teeth. He is taken to the infirmary. In a few days he revives. He is stripped, tied hand and foot. A hammer is raised, first the right leg is broken, then broken again. Then the knee, then the ribs. He is broken up bit by bit.

The real problems Monroy faced, in his prison book and in other writings, dealt with his description of drug traffickers in Nogales and their names. Two of his brothers served as mayors of the city in the seventies, Hector and Octavio (Oscar's twin), and they were allegedly involved with the traffickers he mentioned. Their influence possibly saved his life.

The Mexican prison that Monroy and his anonymous

co-author describe is the school Nacho attended from the age of thirteen onward.

Yes, she says, there was a molest. And her daughter was molested, too. It is far more common than people imagine. I am driving with the radio playing softly as she speaks. The words seem like a discussion of any topic.

"It is far more common than anyone imagines," she repeats.

I have had this conversation before with other women. Just ask! they all seem to be saying, just ask. The Eagles are singing about the problems of American life on the California coast and the details of life in the fast lane. I am driving under the limit.

She seems very much at ease with the subject. I do not know what to say. I never do.

She tells me she had fifty lovers before she had an orgasm.

It is far more common than anyone imagines.

This time the old legal document recounts the murder of a public official. Several guards begin to move through the cells of the prison in Nogales. One, Manuel G., grabs a young inmate. The other prisoners become restless—they sense he is going molest the boy. Nacho strikes at the guards in an effort to free the boy—he is tear-gassed in the face. The guards shut the area down and Nacho retreats. He is seen in a while leaving the prison dining hall with a knife and he shouts to the guard who grabbed the boy, "The end of this blade will be in your back." They take him to the infirmary and hook him up to an I.V. Nacho notices five or six guards hitting another convict, El Chango. He struggles to get up, the guards beat him and give Nacho more gas. Nacho throws water in El Chango's face, pulls a knife, and flings it at the guards. He misses. He regains the knife and plunges it into Manuel G.'s back. Nacho is sentenced to Islas Tres Marias. The judge notes that one must be at least eighteen for the Islas but, because of Nacho's criminal nature, he is going to make an exception in his case. He is barely fifteen years old. The order is eventually changed and he is sentenced to serve his time in Nogales.

I move into the dusk on the edge of town, the place where the bulldozers run on into the night. My weariness has overtaken my mind and I am sinking. We walk up into the foothills, she is anxious to show me her secret places. I am full of tired language—the water table will be gutted, the desert raped, the American empire will flounder in the dry lands. I hear the words and wonder at the banality of my thoughts. On the next ridge a Caterpillar grinds away, bright lights aiding the gouging of the earth in the growing darkness.

The woman shines with smiles but her words are full of regrets. Soon she wonders if the javelina will come to her patio, if the game will flee the explosion of new neighbors. We climb a rock slope, I look down, and a desert tortoise stalls by my foot. The beasts can live a century and I wonder if this specimen is finishing off its hundred years of the American West or sallying forth into the threatening skies of the twenty-first century. The tortoise retreats into its shell and sits there passively waiting for our ugly presence to move on. It is designed, I think, to weather adversity.

We are not. We wince at the sound of the bulldozer but say little. We are tired of saying foolish things but we seem incapable of not feeling them. Every sunrise there seems less left and we know it, but still we bite our tongues. I look over at her and her face is a calm mask but her body is not relaxed. The grunts of the machine continue, the ping of the blade smashing a rock spikes the dusk. She suddenly turns and begins to run through the desert. She is very light on her feet and never brushes against a cactus. I watch her vanish over a rise.

Later we return to her small place, a few rooms tucked away in the mesquite and palo verde with a huge jojoba just out front. We sit in the warm night, drink wine, and wait for coyotes that never howl. It is time to flee town and go to ground.

Four coyotes cross the San Pedro River in the early morning light, pause briefly, drink the cool waters, and pad on. Behind them the San Manuel smelter belches smoke into the blue sky. I got here a day ago and I'm still more in the city than anywhere else. I'm on the run and this is my instant sanctuary. Just up the hill, behind the tailings fanning out from the mine, the dutiful company town sits like a dull industrial jewel. Thousands of feet beneath me men hack at rock to wrest traces of copper from the earth. I am squatting by a major source point for all that acid rain that terrifies fish in Canada. Once a Greenpeace member climbed the great stack in one of those episodic jolts some people deliver to the media in the hope the citizenry will notice the death of the sky. Last night a screech owl called from a nearby saguaro and downriver a baby great horned owl whined for food.

The others are rising now, I can hear the coughing, soft muttering, the music human beings make as they emerge from dreamland and lurch into one more day. Soon the work will begin. We are a mixed bag of state game and fish

personnel, Bureau of Law Management folk, a crazed falconer, and a couple of kids hooked on the call of the wild. I
smell breakfast in the heavy river air.

The falconer tells me he lives in a Phoenix apartment
with a redtail hawk. The bird must be worked several
times a week to keep its hunter's eye. So, early in the
morning he goes to the city's arboretum, a tract filled with
rare plants and succulent leaves. There he has permission
to hunt. For a hour or two the hawk nails rabbits. And
then the man takes it home to its cage, and joins the traffic
and work of the Sunbelt city.

We set up the trap—a mist net strung across the stream
and for bait a great horned owl is tied to a log. When he
hunts in the night, his prey is helpless in the blackness. But
they remember him, the swish of the wings, the sharp talons, and in the light of day if he is spotted, they will attack
with pleasure. The yellow eyes stare impassively, the head
swivels tracking us as we move. The big predator is naked
now and all along the river he is hated. His silhouette
means death to songbirds, hawks, kites, falcons, rats,
mice, snakes. He is doom sweeping out of the night skies
and this makes him the target for the fury of voices rising
in the nearby cottonwoods and mesquite.

I walk the woods. Higher up the mesquite takes over
completely. Little huts dot the forest, strange shelters with
stick walls and stick roofs. The structures look part hogan,
part Mexican hut, and stand in the grove as the imprint of
a distant and fantastic culture, perhaps an old encamp-
ment of Easter Island's monolith builders, perhaps the
home of local trolls. In the shadow of the forest floor the
scene comes straight from *Grimm's Fairy Tales.* The small
shelters are the work of Mexican illegals who toil here as
woodcutters for a nearby rancher. The men are gone now,
the slashed mesquite bleed sap at open wounds. All along
this river the forests are being slain and alfalfa is taking
the ground.

He lives through the telephone. It is 10:00 A.M. and the calls flood in from around the city, the talk never stops, and the talk is deals. He is a hundred years deep into Tucson, his family roots twine back into conquistadores, and he spends his every waking moment selling out the ground under his past, present, and future.

A few months back his fee for ramming a real estate deal through the city government ran to $80,000. He summered on the coast off that one. Now he is busying refilling his coffers. There is this ground west of town that always floods and is worthless, but he and the boys have noticed that a new big canal will act like a buffer dam protecting the land from wild sheets of water and they see millions in the virgin tracts. He scurries about lining up options here and options there, the conversations punctuated with jokes, laughter, and darts of numbers. He is the wildlife of my desert now.

He is about to go hunting at an exclusive lodge in Sonora and shows me his Parker shotgun. I am moved by the beauty and craftsmanship of the weapon and struck by his eye for quality.

The phone rings, he disappears into another conversation. A shopping center here, a higher density there, the face smiles into the receiver, the voice rises and falls, barks and wheedles, teases and snaps. He is alive on the phone. I do not have to hear the party on the other end—the message is always the same, get this through, let's have a done deal. He is a man who always has new jokes to tell you, a running part of his amusement with life. He is laughing now and asks, "Did you hear the one about the guy whose wife was acting funny? Well, he takes her to the doctor and the doc looks her over and say, 'She's either got Alzheimer's or AIDS.' The husband says, 'Christ, what should I do?' And the doc says, 'Well, on your way home stop the car about five miles from the house and kick her out. Then go home and wait. If she shows up in a few hours, don't fuck her.'"

I laugh. This is the story we all apologize for and then laugh at.

I sit on the sofa as he works the phone call by call. Somewhere out in the smog of the city men wait with cement trucks, bulldozers, stakes, pipes, bricks, wires, blueprints. They wait for these calls to finish, for the deal to be a done deal. And then they will move.

There is never enough money, nor will there ever be enough. The expenses can be surprising—tickets and a suite at the Superbowl. Special golf tournaments in distant states. New cars, additions on the house, dinners at serious restaurants with limited menus. The house on the beach safe from the breath of a desert summer.

I sip my coffee from a clear glass cup, he looks over at me beaming as his patters pours into the receiver. I like him. He knows who he is. He is at work and the work seems never to end.

When I was in high school we would drive over the pass between the mountains, a rutted dirt road, and drop down into these thorny glens. The girls would be excited—ah, wilderness. At first they would act circumspect and then relax. The trees seemed to sanction life. We would drink beer, fumble with brassiere hooks. The car radio would boom rock 'n' roll. Once I was here during a flood and the bridge blew out like a toy. I waded naked out into the brown water. The force was monstrous, my knees buckled, and I marveled at the united fury of billions of drops of rain. We made love on the grass, our bodies covered with sticky mud.

Yesterday, I walked these same woods with the director of the state's BLM office. His plane landed at 4:00 P.M., he was chauffeured to the spot, and disappeared into the thicket, a slow-moving, thoughtful man in Levis, boots, and a clean shirt. He carried a detailed map in his hand. Various blocks of garish color marked an insane checkerboard of ownership: federal, state, private, Forest Service,

BLM, surface rights, mineral rights, and so forth. It seemed to me that all the grasping hands of the planet had converged on this one faltering stand of trees. The cry of a gray hawk knifed through the grove. And we all fell silent.

The federal man inspected and thought about two parcels that the BLM might seek in a land swap to protect gray hawks that nest here. There are but sixty pairs of the birds in the United States and fifty-five of them nest in Arizona, mainly along the San Pedro River. They specialize in the murder of lizards and move with grace through the burning air. The federal man specializes in land and over the past few years he has brought 150,000 acres of Arizona river and stream under federal protection. I once met with him in his Phoenix office, the usual sterile government cell. He was the compleat bureaucrat, the soft-spoken warrior of a thousand memos, study plans, meetings, jargon-riddled statements. Out his window spread a world of total cement and smog. Down the street a bleak bar offered women who did not wear clothes. Inside the office the talk was of mystical places we call wilderness because we don't really know what to call them at all.

I now live in a world where soft-spoken bureaucrats are allies. I have given in to the ways of my times.

The stairway is lined with framed letters from politicians who have benefited from the man's advice. He is forty, successful at the advertising business, and now ready to flex his muscles in other arenas, places like elections. Once he worked with the poor in New York City. Once he wrote poetry and won prestigious prizes. He is dressed perfectly, the shirt sewn onto his body, the trousers without a wrinkle, the shoes polished and never marred.

He tells me he likes his creature comforts and for that reason decided to leave poetry for selling. On the wall is a poster: POVERTY SUCKS. He is disappointed in people who oppose the future, who naysay the boom of the Sunbelt.

They are not realistic, he notes. He figures things will be fine for fifteen or maybe twenty years. Then, he is not sure he will want to live here.

I listen with my mind intent on making a record. I do not judge. There is no point. Some things are, some things exist. His desk is spotless and out the window the grubby city sprawls and mutates into new forms of money. Sometimes I wish to curse this conversation and men in his business. I want to denounce the fact that I am mired in a civilization that lives by killing land, an act that will surely in the end kill the civilization itself. But I do not raise my voice. There is no satisfaction for me in such an act. I simply try to understand. And the hard part is not the understanding. Greed is an easy act to comprehend. It is the flutter of my own appetites when the talk spins on about yachts, summer at the beach, tennis at the club, automobiles that move swiftly from zero to sixty and then keep going toward one sixty. I want to strike out but all I see is myself. My face looks warped, like the image in the circus funhouse.

The voice is a model of control, a slow-speed voice so that everyone must alter to his rhythm, to his control. Now he faces a decision. Two people wish to be governor of the state. No one wants either, but they both want it. He must pick between their two campaigns: which one should he run? I ask him how he will decide. He says he will go to work for a million dollars.

And then we talk about tennis.

We stumbled through the brush and trees, the gray hawks kept their calling, and at 7:00 P.M. the federal man flew back on his plane to Phoenix. That night we ate elk, venison, and javelina. The owl refused the shank of a jackrabbit.

I laid out under the stars, the moon stroking the plume of smoke from the smelter. I awoke at 4:30 A.M. and watched a great blue heron flap slowly upstream. Behind me the tailings of mine oozed downhill, a tongue of white powder that will never sustain life. It is something that belongs deep in the earth, but we have not let it be. The gray hawks were silent in their eyrie as I drank bitter, dark coffee from a tin cup.

I live in the basic American insane asylum. Upstream a ways, in the little hamlets hidden by the trees, drug dealers operate their businesses. Here and there in the stripped bottomlands, rich people play with ranches and ride good horses in the fresh morning air. Further on Mormons cling to the nineteenth century, and past them the military operates a base devoted to intelligence gathering. And then comes Mexico and all the hungry eyes.

Somehow the gray hawks have navigated through this human display and found nesting sites. Once they lived over the mountain along the now dead streams that gird Tucson. One April day in 1892 a Major Bendire witnessed courtship, the male and female circling and darting through the forests along the river. "To my ear," the major decided, "there was something decidedly flutelike about these notes. After they were paired they became silent."

The man is fifty-something, very fit, a former national-level hockey player. Now he is a major developer trained up in the Phoenix market and moving in on the possibilities of Tucson. We sit at a table in the trailer while outside big machines rearrange the desert for a retirement community. The sky is brilliant, his voice is smooth and sure, and he is very calm. I ask if the men tearing around outside see wildlife on the site. He says they do. I ask if that is a selling point for buyers.

He says, "I can't sell coyotes."

We talk for half an hour or more. He never smiles, not once.

He tells me he loves his work.

The gray hawks left the streambeds around Tucson in the 1940s as the growing city ate the forests and paved the floodplains. This was the message screaming from the brightly colored slabs on the federal man's map. Property. His calm hand held thousands of shrill voices shouting about complicated patterns of ownership, dreams of the big killing. Nobody ever really tried to get rid of the gray hawks, most people never knew they were there. Perhaps now and then folks picknicking along the streams caught a part of their call, a burst likened by some to the scream of a distant peacock, and momentarily wondered what throat could make such a sound. The birds left in an off-handed manner. A slight silence fell on the forests and then over the years the forests fell also. Now I stand by the banks of the San Pedro and watch a doe drink from the river and then walk off. I still see the map glowing in my head.

A hawk goes for the owl, hits the mist net, and everyone runs. Pictures are taken for the record, the government is hungry for documentation. But this hawk is not a statistic. The talons nick my palm, the body heat boils off the bird into my fingers. The eye is a terrible thing, a brown so dark as to be almost black, and focused totally on a vision of the river I can barely guess. The feathers are fine, perfectly etched, the color a rich broth of gray. Fine black hairs outline the yellow mouth and the black, curved bill with a pink tongue flicking nervously within. I grip the legs tightly in my unease and wonder at the heat. Birds are just a smudge on the edge of my world of cement, steel, and machines.

The hawk is released, swoops across the river, sits briefly on the limb of a dead tree and eyes its recent cap-tors. Then the form lifts off and darts into the shelter of the forest. We begin to disband and return to our separate centers of concrete.

By evening I am standing in the checkout line at a Safeway in Tucson. I feel centuries, millions of years away from the world of the hawks. The man in front of me has a beard and headband, and staring up from his arm are tattoos of the Devil and the face found on packets of Zig-Zag cigarette papers. Big sunglasses hide his eyes but his cheek bears the blue letters SS. His mouth is a hard line and the body is thin and tight. The skin is very pale. He is a rarity also, but not nearly so rare in my city world as the gray hawk.

I am wearing a Hawaiian shirt.

He says, "You don't smell like a gardenia."

My head is full of gray hawks and this does not seem like the best time to launch a discussion on personal hygiene. I gaze off at the magazine rack and catch the headline:

BABOON BOY TAKEN CAPTIVE

Yes, absolutely correct. I think back and imagine I can still feel the heat flaming off the blood of the free bird.

The café sits on the south side of town and all the customers are Mexicans. The help speaks no English, save a woman who just got out of the Army and is scraping by until something good turns up. A couple of the long tables are jammed together and a family, young and old, spreads out to celebrate a birthday. I order a shrimp dinner and settle back. The room is bright walls and bottles of beer.

The blond woman comes in with self-assurance, walks up to the man in his twenties whose birthday is being celebrated. She begins to dance, her dress huge with a balloon she claims is his baby. She slowly strips off her clothes until she is down to a G-string. Her body has landed somewhere in its late thirties but is holding on, her face confronts the miles more honestly. She is thrusting her hips into his face, swinging her breasts close to his eyes. He tries to laugh and then complies with the required discomfort. The women in the family gathering smile tightly and steal looks at the stripper. The men stare directly.

When it ends, she quickly leaves.

I drive north and pass the house with all the bars on the window. He lives there, a man who has made his fortune. Inside I see two men on ladders working on the fresco. All around the house are small homes of poor Mexicans. The man's mother lives down the block in one, she is a *bruja*, a witch. He came to Tucson when he was a teenager, slept under bridges, learned the ropes.

They say now he keeps a wildcat in his house, and has survived fifteen attempts on his life. He is always making deals, complicated deals on both sides of the border. A friend talks to him from time to time and the man says sometimes his phone bill runs $1,500 a month. He is very busy. He cannot read or write. But he can deal, and this city is the place for such a man and such work.

NACHO

I am sitting in a singles' bar drinking red wine with a man who talks of parrots. This particular species has vanished for decades, shot out by feather freaks trying to make an honest buck. And now as the century grinds toward a finale, they are back, released by the state government in a valiant effort to restore the region to the biological richness it once possessed.

The man explains that the birds are moving from mountain range to mountain range and no one knows where they will go or if they will even stay. Perhaps, this place no longer has the look of home to them, perhaps we have done too much to the land to deserve this small return to Eden.

He is talking into his drink, the eyes tightly focused, the words clipped, snapped off from some original source within him and flung down at the top of the polished wooden bar. I can barely hear him, it is Friday night and the saloon is full of males and females looking for the perfect companion for the black hours ahead. Music plays loudly and voices shatter all around us with brittle desires.

The parrots fascinate me. They are from Mexico and have been brought north. They have the proper papers.

I know the talk will not stay with parrots. This Nacho thing, he snorts, you've got to get off it. You forget what people want, who they really are. No one cares about such trash. No one.

I begin to argue and then suddenly stop.

Perhaps you are right, I offer. Perhaps. Maybe I should stick with parrots. I hear the chatter in the forest, see the sheen on the green wings, the thick curve of the beak. It makes a kind of sense to me. Parrots are not ugly and they never put a screwdriver to your throat. There is nothing I can say to him about Nacho—the windy explanations of journalism have nothing to do with me and I am incapable of prattling about the public's right to know, the duties of professionals, the hard ethics of the trade. I believe none of these things. I have but one thought: The parrots are rare and because of the changes in the region it is doubtful that their return will last. They will flash against the sky for a few weeks or months or even years and then the forests will fall still once again. Nacho has always been here and never will be endangered because we carry pieces of him within us. But I say none of these things.

I spin around on my bar stool. The man softens his words. He wanted to deliver a message, and now he has delivered it, but he has no desire to go beyond this friendly piece of advice. We have another drink.

The parrots he says must be photographed in color. They are too rich in plumage for a black and white image. They move in flocks chattering through the trees. They're back now at least for a while. They have returned to *El Norte*.

Lupita rummages around in her head for more memories. Her eyes tell me that my questions baffle her. What is it I want?

"It was after escaping the Islas," she says, "that he came to my home in Tucson and I took him in.

"He would be around the house. He hardly watched TV, he'd just go to bars and make trouble. He didn't know how to stay home and watch TV. Sometimes he liked uppers—you know, like coke—he always wanted to be on the go. He couldn't stay put.

"He would talk to me about what he did. I once saw him take a scissors apart, take the screw out, and then he would take both pieces and leave. He used a scissors to kill with, or a screwdriver. But he said he had to do it. People owed him money. He told me he had killed whole families—the man, the woman, the children—because they owed him money. He killed twenty-eight or thirty-eight, I don't remember. When he killed, he took downers. He had trouble talking about it, he just looked down at his feet and said it hurted him. I never saw him with a mean face."

I have long finished my breakfast but somehow Lupita continues to make hers last, picking at this scrap and that scrap.

"Did he ever say how his work made him feel?" I ask.

She glances up.

"He told me he wished he never did it but he had to take care of his own skin. If he didn't do it, they'd do it to him. I always felt that if he didn't have something to stab with, he was nobody. And he knew he was nobody. If he had a gun, he couldn't hit nothing. He wasn't much of a fighter. I took two men away from him who were trying to beat him."

> *Tell me if the lovers are losers,*
> *In the dust, in the cool tombs.*
> *—Carl Sandburg*

I am spoonfeeding him carrots as he sits in his highchair. Then he tackles peaches, and an oatmeal mush. The bottle of formula is the chaser. He talks to himself now and the eyes track me as I move around the room.

When he awakens, he chatters along for a half hour before demanding that his attendants appear and deliver life's delights. He laughs at the sound of car keys, puzzles out dogs as they glide by on the floor. He notices television but watches me. I am seated at the computer, he is eye-to-eye with me in his chair, the screen flashes by, the printer hums. He takes it all in. I am now a captive trapped in another body, a prisoner of a new double helix.

The eyes gleam, the smile is always at ready. What do we do to them? Did we all start this fresh? My thoughts are very basic and typical. I want him to come out whole. No tumbling down the hill, no bricks flying through the air at his head. But I dismiss these thoughts. The Nacho of the streets is easily branded as a psychopath or sociopath. There is nothing to learn from him. He is the criminal. He did not have the proper highchair as a child.

Finally, I rise and say I have to leave.

She says why?

There are things I must do.

We have been sparring for days about the story. He shakes hands and mumbles gruff greetings when we first meet at Organ Pipe Cactus National Monument. Then, he warms for a day by the crater in the Pinacate, a volcanic wilderness in Sonora, and marches me through the archeology of early man, the way to spot a chopper, the look and feel of the chipped edge, the intricacies of dating objects by desert varnish. He points out the grave of an old one he has never dug up and never will. The green lip of a half-buried grinding stone pokes through the soil; this too he refuses to take.

Later, I decide to walk from Papago Tanks to Sykes Crater. I sense I have committed a serious error: I have acted like a backpacker in his desert. That night he throws a steak on the mesquite coals, a steak he has let hang, age, and grow moldy, and I whip out a tiny stove and heat water for a freeze-dried dinner. We are clearly two nations. I figure there may be no recovery.

We sit at night around a fire, me scribbling on a pad of paper. He scowls at my note taking. I have been admonished to write only of the archeology and dammit, to get it straight. He will not be made to look a fool in print by a scribbling idiot with a backpack. There will be an article, his secrets will be made dots of ink in some magazine. I am the thief come to steal decades of knowing. The archeology, this material we both know is not at issue. I do not care about such things. The theories, dates, disputes, shelf after shelf of artifacts, are musty clues we will never sort out with our science. What we will learn is what we see, hear, taste, smell. He has swallowed decades here and that is what I want. And what he resists.

I watch his moves, listen to his words—no easy task since he swallows half of them and mutters the rest. His hands are strong and pick things up with force, fingers moving together with the bite of a pliers. The sky is black, there is a light breeze and the teasing hint of rain that will not come to this dry ground. I want his fucking mind and it is not there for the asking. It never is in the deserts. The guidebooks, the volumes of lore and tips, all these texts are a screen, a dodge. The real stuff is only spoken, and seldom spoken at that. To know the country you must go into it, and wander, and maybe, just maybe, after the wandering another wanderer will toss down a drink and squint over at you and say a few words. Of course by then, they can be spoken because you already know and the words offered are merely a gesture of confirmation. In my bones, I realize this fact, but still I wait anxiously, always hoping for the shortcut, the tip, the revelation.

A photographer circles in the darkness with his tripod and camera. The shutter snaps; the man stares sternly into the flames.

Behind him stand his real goods: a folding cot, a sleeping bag made from a discarded piece of military canvas, a Coleman stove bought in 1934, a Leica camera obtained in the early thirties, a 1957 Travel-all that has rumbled over the lava beds for a quarter century.

I have heard of him for years, the modern nomad who wanders alone in the black rock. He is a possible key for me, perhaps a model for unraveling my own life. I want roots, I cannot stop wandering. I have never left my country—there has been no Europe, Africa, Asia, no deep blue sea. But I wander, walking, driving, moving, never getting anywhere but always heading somewhere. My house is a shambles, I cannot maintain it. When I walk, I cannot abide a tent. I lie in bag cold and alone, but will not make a fire. These things I cannot explain. He is a key.

Around midnight, he stands, tosses down another shot of mezcal, stares into the flames, and snorts, "I don't give a fuck what you write."

I am home safe. Julian Hayden has said hello.

He is in his seventies and has the moves of an old lion. The tall, lanky body has the carriage of man who has used his muscles. The close-cropped silver hair glows against the tanned skin and chest hair flares from the top of his shirt. He speaks in a monotone and at first the words seem like the product of some foreign language. Then the rhythms become apparent and whole sentences appear—sentences stated in a courtly turn of phrase. The smile comes easily and often and has the look of a grin on the Cheshire Cat. He wears old clothes. He likes old things.

The house is adobe, built after World War II when he finally settled in Tucson with his wife and kids. He had the only jackhammer in the city (bought off a prospector near Yuma, he says) and went into the excavating business. Earlier he had done digs on Hohokam and Anasazi sites, carved silver jewelry for Lord & Taylor in New York, knocked about. There is the time he worked on a freighter, scattered shards of trips on a motorcycle in the late twenties. Bits and pieces appear in conversation; no résumé is ever presented.

I start stopping by at the mud house just off Speedway.

The traffic roars a block away, a chic athletic club squats across the street with handball courts and devoted squash players. Julian is walled off by a grove of mesquite. Lizards huff and puff on the tree limbs, doves come to the fountain. He keeps a slingshot handy to convince visiting cats to hunt elsewhere. The patio is brick, the table old, the lawn chairs aluminum frames with rope laced across to replace the failed plastic strips. A lot of people stop by, the patio functions as a kind of salon for Sonorans, aficionados of the Pinacate, archeologists, yarn spinners, writers, geologists, cranks, citizens, fellow fans of mezcal.

The house is books. Walls of books, books piled up on tables, chairs, everywhere. Classical music plays. There is no television; he does not approve. The reading is fast and loose: Louis L'Amour cheek to jowl with technical archeological papers, Larry McMurty atop a study of early cave paintings. Downstairs are more books. If you want to talk books, sit down. If you want to talk television, go away.

It is very difficult at first to understand the artifacts. Everything seems to have a meaning yet nothing is volunteered. Then the painting of the smoke tree in the Mojave becomes a work by his mother's hand. The old photograph over the desk of a woman on a mule is his late wife coming out of the Sierra. In the back off his bedroom is a small room with good northern light where he carves silver and gold. Wooden mallets lie about, racks of chisels and files. He sees things that have been dead for a thousand years, images of birds, frogs, big cranes that have been buried in the earth and resting on the surfaces of old clay pots, or carved out of the pearl white of old shells. These he liberates. He hands me a quivering mass of silver, a series of sandhill cranes doing a mating dance, a thing observed ten centuries ago by someone and now hauled from a desert tomb, carved into silver, and flashing once again in the light of day.

Many things are buried from view. You have to ask the

right question to get the right answer. For months I work on a book about a nearby range, the Santa Catalina Moun- tains. I stop by every couple of days, crack a beer— "You know where they are"—and sit out under the mesquites. The talk rambles—Julian corresponds with Alger Hiss and is a devoted member of the National Rifle Association, so any subject is possible. From time to time, he asks idly about the book. I confess I am puzzled by the lack of Indian lore about the range, just a few scraps on foraging, a Papago story about the origin of their name for the high peak, Frog Mountain, and the idea that Navitcu, a god figure, lives up there.

Julian nods. I drink another beer.

One day I ask him if he knows anything about Navitcu. Well, yes, he says. He goes in the house, rifles his files (I have this vision that somewhere under the mud building is an archive about the size of the Library of Congress), and comes out with his firsthand account of a big ceremony, the last one ever held as it happens. And sure enough there is his watercolor of Navitcu, and it turns out he knew people who portrayed the god, and on and on. I scan the text: it is just after World War II, the dancers move within a great circle of people. A young couple sets their baby on the ground nearby, Julian sketches. Suddenly a dust storm sweeps out of the desert and the sky goes brown. Little drifts of sand begin to pile up around the baby. Julian is concerned. And then the storm ends, the dance continues, night falls. The neat typewritten text spills on page after page. It has snored in his file cabinet for four decades. He tosses down a shot, I look up.

You have to know the right question.

Nothing is volunteered.

In 1956, he decided to go into the Pinacate and study early man. For years, he had let his archeological skills lapse. But now the excavating business was successful, his wife

Helen helped run things, and he could get away. He tells me this out under his mesquites. He is quite aware of his motives: he was in his mid-forties back then and facing the failure of ambitions that men seldom can put a name on. He likes the term "male menopause."

He is insistent about the importance of Helen to his life and work. They met during a Hohokam dig in the thirties. He says he would never have amounted to anything without her. The conventional sentiment has feeling and force when he says it. She has been dead for several years. He writes letters to her at night.

So he goes, weekend after weekend, year after year, hundreds of days in all spent mapping, measuring, examining ancient sites among the lavas. Once a friend and I were stumbling across the lavas and dropped into a wash and discovered what we felt must be a pristine ancient site. We were excited at the thought that at last we had something to tell Julian about the Pinacate. When we got back we told him the location. He disappeared into the house, came out with one of his maps, and showed us the precise spot—neatly marked as a site years before.

He walked the ancient trails, hundreds of miles of them. He became a local legend among the Mexicans. And, because he leaned toward very early dates for man in this hemisphere, a heretic among the scholars. He can talk at length about the esoterica of varnish dating, but these arguments usually pass over my head. Julian discovered a world all his own and he mastered it. Somewhere in the house are numerous artifacts, fat folders of notes.

Once I mentioned a friend was doing a study of the wolf in the Southwest. He disappeared into the house and returned with a note on a wolf sighting decades before. And a photograph with measurements of the track.

He is appalled by my lack of scientific skills, by my ineptness at making detailed notes, serious jottings that get things down to the exact centimeter.

The men at the ranch are all smiles and jokes. He gets out of the old Travel-all and jokes with them. They are lonely against the sand and rock of the Pinacate and busy themselves making cheese. Flies swarm. He leans against a fender and smiles. He is "Don Julian" here, the old one who wanders the *despoblado*. In the Sonoran cafés he flirts with the waitresses. In the ranchos he trades *dichos* with the vaqueros.

The acquaintanceships go back decades and people tend to fall into genealogies in his head. In Sonora, Julian is the alien who is at home.

There is a tradition here of rogue scholars. Carl Lumholtz at the turn of the century went in with a local boy named Alberto Celeya. Malcolm Rodgers, Ronald Ives, and Hayden followed these tracks. And they met and talked to Celeya. A few days ago, Julian exchanged small talk with Celeya's granddaughter—another thread of continuity. It is dusk now and we are camped by a crater drinking mezcal. Rodgers's and Ives's ashes are scattered on a nearby hill. We toast.

It is night, we sit in the dark under the trees and drink. The talk flows, he disappears into the past, a place with few hard dates but with exact names that mean nothing to me and always seem to melt away. A place of appetites, odd moments, fierce hungers. He finds Nacho interesting, he senses the type, the emptiness in the belly. He talks about a man he knew, a drifter on the border who took it into his head to find the fabled *Yaqui* gold and vanished south heading for the Bacatetes, the heart of that Indian nation. Then nothing. He reappears driving a huge car, a Lincoln I think, and flashing money. But says nothing. There is this boy, a boy Julian knows later as a man, and the boy is at a mud house down in Sonora when one night the man with the Lincoln comes roaring up. He has been shot. He cleans his wound and then sends the boy out to his car to fetch a bandage. The boy rummages, finds it, looks a little more and sees a bar of gold, one with an ancient stamp in the gleaming metal. He takes the bandage in, says nothing. The man eventually leaves. And that is it. The tale has no ending. There is no moral. It just hangs there over the country.

Sometimes, at night, he tells tales of the questions the desert does not answer. He is camped in the Pinacate and walks an ancient Indian trail. He notices a badger beating down the trail and follows. Then he notices a redtailed hawk on a saguaro. The badger goes down a hole, the hawk dives to catch what he has scared up. This goes on and on and Julian follows and watches the team. The badger walks up to him and sniffs his boot. The beast's fur glows with health and vigor.

He says that when he first came to the Pinacate the birds flew up to his face, they were so unused to a human presence and so curious about this new mammal. In his talk and in his presence the place becomes a wonderland, one at odds with the exact notations in his fieldwork, with the careful measurements, the complicated debates about dating desert varnish.

There is no contradiction, just two separate ways of perceiving that are operating in one human being.

He is aware of this fact. And late at night under the stars, his interest in the place becomes simple and clear. He comes here to be with early men and women and children. There is something irresistible about a sleeping circle— they seem to demand that a person crawl in and curl up within the embrace of the old stones. He is careful about this attraction—I am shameless in my submission to it— but it is there and he does not let his science make him deny its force and power.

But there is another tale, the best of all I can sense. He is driving out of the Pinacate down a dirt rut and suddenly sees the tracks of two people in the road. He gets out, looks around, finds where the footprints begin, but when he

searches the surrounding desert he finds no trace of them.
The tracks simply begin without warning. He goes on, the
tracks continue. And then suddenly end. He gets out again,
searches, and finds no sign of them leading out. Nor are
there tire tracks to suggest they hopped in a truck for a
ride. So the story ends.

He stays up late into the night and stares into the flames
alone. He sips mezcal. I crash, crawl into my bag, and
drift.

I look over and see him sitting, his back framed by the
glow of the fire.

NACHO

David Perez Diaz is frightened. He knows Nachito has always lusted after his sister. Finally, she left the city of Nogales to be safe. Nacho wanted her to join his group and when she refused, he threatened to kill Perez several times. In October 1985, Perez's sister returns to Nogales. On the night of November 8, he and his sister hear gunshots outside the house. She runs outdoors and screams that it is Nachito. Perez is terrified—he knows of at least two people Robles has killed for much less than this matter of his sister. On November 15, Nacho and his friend El Guero Jipi—"The Blond Hippy"—come to the house. They find Perez with his friend Raul Trejo. Nacho and his *compañero* pull a shotgun and a .38. Nacho spits at Perez, stands before him. He slams a pistol into his stomach, grabs his shirt and shakes him, and says, "Remember I told you before I was going to kill you. Well, today is the day." Perez feels a horrendous shiver pass through his body. He instinctively pulls a .25 from his vest and shoots Robles in the hip and leg. Nacho doubles over and tells Perez, "You motherfucker, you've fucked me. And

you beat me in this shootout." Nacho and Jipi retreat a
short distance, turn, and fire. The bullets miss. They melt
away.

I am sitting at a table in the empty bar on a Sunday night. I
have four hundred pages of legal documents in Spanish
and I wonder if I will ever find my way out of them. The
glasses of wine arrive like clockwork without a sound.

The off-duty bartender sits on a stool. She is very slender
and dead drunk. Her black hair is soft and has a light curl,
the face is thin and full of fine bones and sensitive touches.
She is the kind of woman you expect to write poetry she
never shows anyone, to have cooking skills she seldom has
call to display. A woman who reads thin books and keeps
them in perfect order in a nice white bookcase. I remember walking one day and seeing her go past on the back of
a hog. The guy had his big hands clutched to the controls,
tattoos sparkling on his arms. He was bearded, a little on
the grubby side, and guarded his face with a scowl. She
was wearing a thin white T-shirt and her skinny arms en-
circled him. Her small breasts poked at the white fabric.

Now she is standing by my table, weaving and struggling to focus her eyes. I shove my pile of documents aside
and look up. Her face has the softness of a Jimson weed
blooming on a moonlit night. She begins to talk, the
speech rambling, the words slurred. She asks about my
work, says the heap of Xeroxes looks real interesting, and
she bets it's a lot of fun doing what I do.

I think that if I put my arms around her she will crum-
ble into dust and slowly filter down to the carpet through
the dead bar-room air. It is Sunday night and she is drunk
and she can remember no poems to salvage this situation.
The arms are so thin, she has the look of a child.

I hear her out. There is nothing to say. And then she
stumbles past.

A couple of days later I drop in again. She is blind to me

and acts as if nothing had happened. She bends diligently
over a sink full of glasses behind the bar and washes and
stacks. Her face is much the same but now the eyes have a
hard focus. I look into them and see black wells where the
women live in trailers, the clothes are draped on chairs,
and the men come and go and every once in a while beat
them.

Some things just are and we are trained never to speak
of them. We simply drink through those hours.

The newspaper is yellowing now, its May 1 date fading
into the dust where all newspapers go to die. I reread the
story.

> According to information received both were executed in
> the classic style of the Mafia. At this time it appears that the
> sacrifice may have been vengeance for some of the numer-
> ous crimes committed by "El Nachito" Robles. . . . Neverthe-
> less, at the present time the evidence suggests that El Na-
> chito and his cousin Carlos Enrique Lopez had participated
> in a heavy drug deal and that something didn't come off as
> expected. In the meantime, yesterday in the Pantheon, the
> youth Ignacio Robles was buried after religious ser-
> vices. . . . With the death of El Nachito, it also brings to an
> end the tragic journey of a homicidal youth who was cred-
> ited for various homicides, as many on this border as in
> Tucson, Arizona, where he finally met the end in that form
> that was expected: Violently.

Lupita wants us to know she did not fear. She is a woman
who can take the blows of life. I sit there quietly waiting
for a message.

"Nacho always lashed out suddenly," she explains,
"never gave any warning to the person he was going to kill,
he was a cowardly killer, at least I think so. So when they
tried to scare me about him I told them I was not afraid
because I am always ready for the traitor. I'm a snake, and

like a snake, ready to strike before they attack me because
snakes are treacherous too."

*In the United States there is more space where no-
body is than where anybody is. That is what
makes America what it is.*

— *Gertrude Stein*

The game is changing. My office is dark, the blinds pulled
shut, the afternoon fading. Art is very excited and sits on
the edge of the folding chair clutching the small tape re-
corder in his hands. He has been down on the south side
scouting out more little nuggets of facts and has dropped
by the old dealer's house. They sat in the front yard soak-
ing up some rays and shooting the shit. The old dealer is
not that old, somewhere in his early forties, but in his field
he is an ancient. His hand moves like a ghost through
some seventy killings still sleeping as open cases down at
the police station, a smiling factor in jacket after jacket of
files that never seem to close.

"You gotta listen to this," Art says. "You gotta listen to
this."

I sip black coffee, lean back in my green chair, and turn
from the pile of manuscripts on my official desk, a thirty-
five-dollar folding table. Voices crackle out of the speaker,
men drinking and talking and laughing. I can see the yard,
the dirt raked clean, perhaps a mulberry tree offering a
neat circle of shade, the street strung with old cars, dust on
their dented fenders. They never leave down there, no
matter how much they score. Suddenly a black voice
jumps into the tape, a guy who is walking down the street,
sees the old dealer having a beer, and comes over.

The black voice just got out of the joint an hour ago—
they wanted him to cop a plea, to do five, but he snaps,
"Fuck that, I said, I want a trial." He can do time, that's not
a problem, he's just finished a stretch, but shit, that was
federal. The state's never nailed him, and damned if they
will.

"I don't pimp," the black voice cautions. "I'm a hustler. Cocaine, heroin. But I'm fifty years old, man, I'm tired of hustling."

He's had it. He's gonna sue for false arrest. Sue! You hear me. Get some big bills, make a killing, and then leave Arizona. Every con in the joint is going to leave Arizona, kiss this fucking state goodbye. Shit, yes. Get the hell out and open a business somewhere. Yes.

"Hey, could you loan me five, man?" the voice continues, "just for cigarettes and the bus, man? They wanted me to cop a plea! Fuck that shit."

He's gonna have him a smoke, some beers, and then see the old lady. Shit, who knows what she'll think. They had an argument just before this last bust. But he's out now. Just a five to tide him over for the afternoon, you know, man.

The tape snaps off. Art smiles. It's always out there, his smiles says, always out there. The old dealer, the black guy, everything. The juice. I think, how do we make a story out of this? Low lifes, file under criminals. Art does not care, Christ, just look at his smile. The juice.

I stare into the walls of the office while the black voice fades against the cool white surface.

The woman is getting loaded and her long blond hair hangs down straight and true remembering the sixties when all you needed was love. She is well educated and very gentle in her manner, the kind of person who would never raise her voice or spill tea. Around her the air swirls with the sounds of rock 'n' roll and people circulate seeking other people in the saloon. She is the kind of person you trust with your children.

I am preoccupied. My work has crushed my life. I can barely remember savoring the calm of San Blas, or hearing the cry of a gray hawk. I feel like an empty husk of what I once seemed to have been. A year or so ago, the public safety director in Nogales, Sonora, was mowed down in his office. And I have these damned news clips riding in my coat pocket. A twenty-eight-year-old Mexican guy took a .45 in the head a block from the fence, just up the street from a fancy restaurant where I love to eat shrimp and watch the waiters worship the big guys who come in with pistols on their hips and a squad of companions. The man who takes the bullet in his brain dies. He was a Mexican reporter, but when Art places calls in Sonora, no paper will admit they ever employed him. *"Si,"* one woman explains, "he was a reporter but *not at my paper."* A few days later, details flutter out of the silence. Now the story has him as in the life, the reports suggest his fountain pen contained heroin. The New Journalism hits a new high. Then he vanishes from type and from talk. He is just another stiff in the business.

The other clip is interesting also. For days Art has heard on the streets of south Tucson that something heavy is coming down in Nogales. The little story reports that eighty Federales have descended on the border city to restore order to the community. One man has been slain, nine drug suspects busted. The Federales work for Caro Quintero, the main man, and the arrested and the killed, according to the people on the street, are employees of the Burned Ones and colleagues of the state police. Housekeeping.

The blond woman tells me of her life and it is interesting. All those restless years, the hard things and scrapes that belie her civil countenance and mannered ways. We are confiding the way survivors of the sixties tend to. I tell her of the clips, of Nacho, of my obsession with matters that do not seem to matter in the day-to-day world.

Her eyes listen. The skin is very fair and smooth. She is a woman who always will smell fresh, something about her soul, I suspect. I immediately like her because although her life is likely to a path of ruin, there will be no cruelty. And I sense she will never surrender. I suspect she knows

classical music and can play the piano and makes wonderful breads.

She says, "My grandmother was a prostitute at age thirteen, won in a card game in Yuma."

Something is not being reported, I think.

It is 10:00 A.M. and Art is drinking. He throws down a beer
and winks that it is all part and parcel of the night before.
He is very excited. We are sitting in a coffeeshop and the
table is covered with manuscripts that I am diligently editing. I have come here to be alone and work. This is not to
be.

The room is softly lit and the booths are full of people
drinking coffee, smoking, talking in a low rumble. The
faces are American and the skin a kind of paste that denies
the flesh has pleasures. The manuscript before me considers the plight of a presidential candidate who is low in the
polls, what it feels like back in his hotel room where the
staff argues about what must be done and what he must
say to get the proper attention for his ideas and programs.
He may be the next leader of the United States, it is possible in this nation of endless possibility. I sip decaffeinated
coffee. I am backing away from everything. Art orders another beer. He is seducing me. I am willing.

The old dealer, he whispers, the old dealer is in trouble.
I nod. Remember that body, he continues, the woman
found in the desert with her head cut off and her hands cut
off? Well, that was the old dealer's girlfriend. She welched
on deal and left him hanging for $150,000. So he did that.

"How old was she?" I ask.

"Why? About thirty. So what?"

"I just wanted to know."

The waitress comes by with the beer and gives me another splash of coffee. Art drops his voice and drifts into
deeper codes. Last night his friend came over, you know
who, and they went out and had some beers. The guy was

looking for the old dealer. Art asks why. The guy tells him, well, I've had a $20,000 deposit on a case.

Art smiles. His friend has the contract, he beams, he is going after the old dealer. The people who put up the goods, the $150,000 shipment, want their money. And, you know the head of Homicide, a guy who has known the old dealer since they were boys together on the south side, he called and wanted to know about the old dealer. "Where is he?" he asked. Thinks he can make a case on this one after flubbing the first seventy or so. And a half-dozen guys are looking for him anyway, friends of the headless woman.

Art asks the guy who has taken the case for $20,000 just what he is doing. The guy smiles and said, "Looking for a missing person." Then he shows Art his chromeplated .22 with special cartridges, softpoints with a b-b implanted in the tip. When they hit, the guy explains, the b-b just goes splat and makes you mush.

The guy went back to Art's place with him and made some long-distance calls, all to Mexico. The old dealer has gone south. He must make another deal, earn that $150,-000, or the man with the .22 will be trailing him forever. The friends of the headless woman, the cops, these matters can be attended to in time. But not the man with the chromeplated .22. He has been launched and only big money will return him to earth again.

Art talked for a long time with the guy on the case and now in the coffeeshop he leans forward, talks more. He must tell this. It is so alive. The guy has trouble sleeping at night and drinks a fifth each evening to get him through the dark hours. But when this case came up, he decided to dry out. So he loaded up his horse, got a rifle, bedroll, some pistols, and rode up into the mountains. For three days and nights he shivered and went cold turkey. He punched trees with his fists to wear off the tension. Art saw his hands, all bruised and bashed from punching those trees.

It will be interesting, Art smiles, to see if the old dealer
can come through this one. He has known the dealer all
his life. He is a psychopath, Art beams, the nicest guy you
could hope to meet.

The fellow who has taken the case, the man with those
special cartridges, he is an old friend also. He invited Art
to go along on a business trip. He first will go south and
supervise the pickup of the merchandise. He and Art will
then follow the goods to the East. They will never touch
the merchandise, never get near them. They will just keep
everything in sight to protect the investment. He figures he
will put $22,000 into the deal and triple it in a week or so.

Of course, first he must attend to his missing person
case. He has done such work before. It is just another as-
signment. And it is nothing personal. He knows the old
dealer also. He kind of hopes he comes up with the money,
he likes the guy. It is simply a matter of $150,000. The
headless woman is someone else's concern.

I tell Art I must finish editing the manuscript. The candidate is still in his hotel room wondering if he should focus
more on his plan for changing the nature of the workplace
or stress his record on children's rights. He must learn to
smile more easily, and remake his body language. His staff
is concerned that he will come across as cold and aca-
demic. He has a tendency to do that.

I ask Art if he is going to help the police or the guy on the
case find the old dealer.

He looks at me with amazement.

"How stupid do you think I am?"

Pepe Sierra Intz is a radio announcer in Nogales, Sonora.
Art and I bump into him near the Palace of Justice. He
says, "Nacho? A few days after he died, the cops went to his
family with real gory shots of the corpse. They also
brought them around to the local radio and newspaper
people. They wanted to know if it was really him. I in-

stantly knew it was *El Famoso* because I had covered him so many times."

Art stumbles onto a story about a woman. She did not perform satisfactorily in a deal and Nacho went to visit her. He beat her. And then he took out his knife and cut up her face, and her breasts and her genitals. And then he beat her some more and left her for dead. The police have not been informed of this matter, Art tells me over a glass of wine. The woman, she is alive, she can be found. Perhaps, she will talk.

Yes, I think, that would be good. A visit with Nacho in a second-hand way. But it is over. Yes, over. I drink. Still, I would like to hear the woman's voice and see the knife in her eyes. Perhaps, catch a glimpse of Nachito tumbling down the hill in Colonia Buenos Aires, bricks flying through the air. Smell the tail of the dragon.

She is angry but she masks this feeling with expressions of concern. She has decided that it is hopeless around me. Let us just be friends, she announces. Sometimes, she notes, I can be very nice, and open, and inviting. And then sometimes I just wall everyone off, and seem to shut down as a human being.

"You just change," she sighs, "and then I don't know what you are."

She has studied psychology and this comes into play as she explains me to me. I nod agreement. It is always easier to agree, yes is better than no. Also, I sense what she means. My voice will go flat, emotionless, my words will be simple, polished hard stones strung out like gravel. I will mask my anger with absolute evenness of tone.

I am relieved. It is easier this way. Anything is easier than explaining. So we agree. I am all wrapped up with a ribbon, a finished thing. Case closed. It is far easier this way.

Then she grinds beans and makes coffee and we talk of other matters.

The wake lasts three days down in the small four-room house on Rio Hondo. Lupita only goes for the first day. The custom is for the feet to point toward the door but the room is too small, so the coffin is not in its proper alignment. Men keep vigil, one at each end. "They wouldn't even get close to Nacho when he was alive," she smiles, "but now that he was dead. . . ."

Lupita arrives with flowers. She wears four rings, and carries flowers so as not to appear empty-handed before the family. She stares down at the corpse, all washed, in good clothes, nice looking, the coffin bought for $1,500 in Tucson. Lupita had been through two false death reports before with Nacho and then he would turn up alive.

Lupita asks the corpse, "Is that really you, you bastard? Are you really dead? What happened to your seven lives?"

Art will not give up. We must go back to Nogales, there are these loose ends, all these loose ends that he says bedevil him. But their real function is to stop the thing from ending. The keymaker operates from a 1947 Diamond T truck on a side street. It is a very small business. He drives a nice car, his thick neck is wrapped with gold chains, a bracelet spells out his name with gold and diamonds, and his watch blinds with an array of precious stones. He has a wonderful smile. He knows how to unlock things.

He has known Nacho's dad since childhood and he says some parts of the clan are rich, rich, they own many butcher shops in the city. Ah, the father, he was a man, broad shoulders, and spirit. The son was different, a killer for money and for pleasure. The father never married Nacho's mother, he smiles, she was just one of his women. There is a man who can tell you about the son, tell you much. He will introduce us.

We get in his car and go to the house on a nearby back street. The man we seek is a Mexican cop. The keymaker gets out and walks to the door, knocks, and is speaking to a woman. She says her man has a hangover. They talk some more. The cop will not come out, he will not meet with the gringos, not be seen with them. He is afraid.

I tell Art it is over. Earlier at the police station we could feel the chill in the air. The head man took us in a private room and sat at his desk and was very cold. It is over. We cannot get closer. There are warnings, silent warnings, but they are very loud and clear. Stop asking questions, the warnings say, leave it alone. Then there are warnings that are not silent, messages sent that say, do not continue, do not return to Nogales or we will have to do something about it. It is over.

I am in a bar drinking beers with Art. His face is angry. He keeps ticking off the things we do not have, the loose ends we must tie up. I say, no, it is over. I can smell danger. I want out.

He refuses. The house. He must see the house, and it turns out to be two-storied, a garish green, a sheet covering the door. Art must see the grave, and it is in *El Pantheon de Heroes,* a weed-filled space in the Colonia Buenos Aires. The cross is black iron, the wreath faded purple and white paper flowers. On a foot-long strip of masking name someone has inked the name Ignacio Robles Valencia. The foot of the grave is already eroding.

Art returns to Nogales two days later. He comes alone. There was this one lead about Nacho's aunt, a woman said to operate a small grocery two blocks from the Palace of Justice. He must talk to her, he must. He enters the little *tienda* and two young guys are standing there. The stock is a few cans, some vegetables rotting on a table. Art asks for the aunt. They look at him and ask what is his business. He says he is interested in learning more about Nacho Robles. The two men invite him to the back of the store. They pull out .45 automatics. Art talks very fast and with great, and evident, sincerity.

It is over. Now Art agrees.

The day *La Voz del Norte* reported Nacho Robles's murder, the history column for that date, a regular feature, celebrated a Sinaloan bandit who robbed from the rich and gave to the poor. The column wondered what he could have done with modern machine guns. El Nachos will continue to come forth from the barrios and villages. All ingredients are present: the market, the wages, the pleasures. They will flourish as long as North Americans will pay good money for crops that South Americans and Mexicans can produce. There are no *corridos*, Mexican ballads, about Nacho to date; perhaps, in time, he can be transformed from a sociopath into lore. He has certain useful ingredients: he inspired fear, he escaped poverty, he did not give in, and he died violently.

The life simply continues. About two months after Nacho went down, another execution took place in Tucson. They happen fairly regularly, making the newspapers gritty tombstones of dry facts. This killing was of small moment, merely another tiny flicker in the industry.

Not many came to the funeral of Angel Martinez, just some family and ten or twelve friends. He was thirty-one years old. At 12:30 A.M. on Monday, June 25, he went with a friend to a house on North York Place in Tucson to buy drugs. While making the deal there was a knock on the door and a man asked for Angel, who then went outside, closing the door behind him. A few minutes later, the people in the apartment heard a popping sound and after a couple of minutes they went outside and found Angel in the front yard with a bullet hole behind his left ear.

Larry Martinez, Angel's brother, acknowledges that his brother was a dealer and an addict. He says he came north illegally two years ago and worked in Tucson as a gardener and landscaper. He dreamed of making big money. Soon he was dealing and eventually worked his way into a drug gang on the west side of town.

Angel's body is decorated with tattoos. On his left breast

the nickname "Licho," on his neck and chest spider webs, the Virgin of Guadalupe on his left forearm, and underneath that a heart, a star, and the name "Lydia." His right arm sports a naked woman with the wings of a butterfly.

On his left hand is the inscription, *"Mi Vida Loca,"* My Crazy Life.

Sometimes he cries in the night and she gets up and walks the floor with him. I always sleep right through the cries. I have always slept well and deeply and marvel at this fact. Once as a child electricity followed the powerline into the farmhouse and blew the circuit box above my head into flame and smoke. And still I slept. In the dark hours I make a peace with myself.

I think of a new fact Art has turned up from the streets. Namely, that Nacho was in the habit of cutting a strip of skin off his victims. A kind of trademark.

The baby is beginning to teeth and the pain wakes him and disturbs him, so he cries. It is normal, I tell her, and she nods. But she must comfort him. She cannot just let him cry. He must be held.

Perhaps she is right.

I think: Soon he will have teeth. And begin eating meat.

I drink black coffee and decide it is time to decide.

The dog died a month ago. He was almost ten years old. I originally found him through a small classified ad, a Great Pyrenees for sale for such-and-such a price at the following address. I wondered how such a big dog could appear before the public in such tiny agate type. The man who answered the door was wearing his colors, the arms rich with tattoos. His colleagues lounged about the tumbledown house on a frayed edge of town. He walked me out to the yard where the huge white dog was chained. He was eight months old and had been through four owners. The man, sporting a Harley hog grin, said the animal had been collected from a guy who had failed to properly pay a debt to the fellows in the club. The dog was listless, the gaze unfocused, the sun burning in the shadeless yard. He limped from a wrenched shoulder. I went over and patted him on the head. He showed no reaction. I looked into his face and saw the craters of convict eyes.

I bought him. He was indifferent to me. When we walked into the house, he strolled out into the backyard, sniffed around, and went to sleep under a shade tree. Things begin to disappear. I hang my clothes on a peg at night and find my billfold filched from my trousers in the morning. He does not bury such items deeply. Then, with time, he begins to leave the goods by the back door, then the hallway, then by my sleeping head. He sleeps all day, patrols all night. I awaken in the black hours and feel this massive head softly breathing over my face, then hear the footfalls slowly pad away. He never licks. It is not something his breed relishes.

This goes on for years. He is very diffident and only if I leave for weeks on trips does he revolt. As soon as he sees the backpack on the floor, he disappears into the sanctuary of his yard and has no more commerce with me. I return and find my bed fouled with dirt and leaves. I go out into the yard and he stares at me silently and offers no apology. He adopts the cats and they begin to sleep near him. I can hear their silent bodies drinking some deep beverage of security. Once he sleeps near the screen door when two German shepherds suddenly chase a cat into the front yard. The dog rises like a white ghost, goes through the screen. The first shepherd he grabs by the neck and sends airborne. The second flees into the street and quails between the legs of the woman who had been jogging with them. I race out and see a look in her eyes that says she has accepted death. But nothing further happens. The huge white dog stops at the edge of the sidewalk, apparently the border he has assigned to his turf, stares for a moment, then turns and goes back into the house. And falls asleep. He is an animal who offers no explanation and makes no complaint. Sometimes I am gone for hours or days and come home and find him asleep in the front yard. He has opened the door with his mouth and gone out to check.

Finally, the years add up, and he begins to fail, sleep more, and then I find the tumors. There is nothing left but the dying. He has used up his time. I come home late one night in December, I have been at a political party in the foothills with catered food, booze-slurred talk, and the nervous scanning by eyes that count votes. A woman has pressed against me as we drink in a roomful of people, she keeps talking television and moving closer while her husband stands with his back turned a few feet away. The air is stale.

I find him slumbering on the patio. The breathing comes heavily. Near dawn he surrenders, hemorrhages blood out his mouth, and vanishes into time. I wrap the body in a blanket and carry him out. He feels like a man with his flopping weight of a hundred twenty-five or thirty pounds.

For thirty hours, I drink.

The cat avoids that spot on the patio for days and days. And now she is slipping away.

Her nose is half gone, a gouge streams inward toward her skull and displays the jagged edge of a canyon carved in flesh. The cat eyes remain alert, and at this very moment seem to lack apprehension. The doctor examines her and sighs. I wait for the message. Last night she could not breathe, the problem with the nose had reached some kind of limit, and she pressed against me and I held her into the dawn. The wheezing came in sputters, fluid sprayed against my face, the body shuddered with a new understanding of the end.

The fur is dull and flat-looking and there seems no hope of the fine sheen returning. Yet she still eats, devouring her cat food. The doctor says there is no chance and we might as well end it. So we do.

It is a small death, the cat weighs but nine pounds. We have been together for years but the years have been brief instants. A howl in the morning demanding that the food dish be filled. A leap onto the lap for a moment of attention. I leave and am gone a week or two or three and

return to find my bed covered with feathers and the remains of her kills. I sense I should have some quick,
contained reaction to killing her.

I do not. A flicker in the long night.

Drive, just drive, I think.

Anna's picture stares down at me from the wall. She is
frozen forever in the summer heat of Brawley, California.
The breasts hang heavily in her swimsuit and the face is
open and yet closed. I eye her sensuous large lips formed
in a shape that is not quite a frown but clearly a warning. A
towel is draped off her shoulder as if she has just had a
work-out at her favorite spa, and behind her a woman's
face is painted on an old wall with the word *"Mujeres."*
Anna's eyes focus hard on something outside the frame of
the photo and they seem powerful enough to look through
a thousand years.

Normally, she works until 10:00 P.M. and the baby sitter
costs ten dollars an hour. Last summer she worked in the
packing sheds.

I can feel the 114-degree heat of the Imperial Valley. I
lean forward toward her and ask, "What do you want to
do?"

She hesitates and thinks about this question. Her eyes
admit nothing.

"I don't know," she says softly, "I don't think there is a
magic button that goes bang."

She gives me her address.

I can hear her voice. It is quiet, almost soft, but with
edges that slash in and out of her sentences. Sometimes
late at night I wonder if she is dead, or if she has been cut
up. I can feel the heat of the small town Saturday night.
When I peer into her face she is never moving, she can
never move. But she is never silent. The voice talks inside
my head. I cannot make out the words but I always understand the intent.

The plane lifts off and the nose aims toward the heavens. My stomach churns because I am not at ease. I sat up most of the night thinking of the dead cat. I could feel no guilt, just failure. And yet, I cannot understand why I feel failure. Things live and then die. I stare down at the city and watch the small houses march across the land in sturdy rows. The desert begins and I delight in the brown dirt and the thin green outlines of the arroyos stitching across the bajadas and dusty flats. The flight becomes a trance, the engine drones, the land streams below, the horizon slowly crawls toward us. There is very little to do, the machine seems to fly itself. After an hour we are over Gila Bend.

The ear plugs dilute the cries of the engine and stop the danger of talk.

The walls are covered with ghosts. There is the smiling face of a Mexican child with crooked teeth. Or the road map of San Blas. The hard stare of Nacho.

The truck breaks down. I decide to walk to work and then give up and pay my fare. The bus driver laughs and says this is his thirty-second wedding anniversary and he'd better hit the malls tonight after work and pick up something for the old lady. His face is worn but carefree. He has lived here for decades and as the town boomed and the land roared upward with value, he profited not at all. He does not seem discontented with this fact. He is busy thinking of his anniversary and the quick evening hunt through the malls for some token. I listen to his chatter and watch the cords of his neck flex through the deep creases of fat flesh.

"Thirty-two years," he smiles, "and maybe ten good nights."

I am at a loss.
   I cannot stop leaving.
   I cannot keep out of the various morgues.

I feel the bones snapping in my body.

I am in Toni's Place, a Mexican bar in the Imperial Valley. Roberto is forty-three years old and does farm work when he can find it. He has five children and many teeth missing. We drink beer and he laughs easily. He barely speaks English, I pretend to speak Spanish. On the back bar is a shrine to the Virgin of Guadalupe and nearby two portraits of John and Robert Kennedy.

He is very reluctant to smile because of the broken teeth. Roberto's cap states: "You Should Have Seen the One That Got Away."

The air flows across the desert and barely moves the burro weed and brittle bush. The plane sits rigid, an aluminum icon in a pan of dirt. She smiles, and off the water comes the odor of rotting fish. I drink a cup of wine.

There was her small town high school reunion in Michigan and she went. They all gathered in a building and danced and talked and sized up the miles in each other's eyes. People slept with the people they had desired in high school but failed to approach. The class hero, the star of the football team, the president of student body, he never showed up. Afterwards she learned he had sat in the parking lot in his car and watched the people come and go. He did not leave the darkness, he just watched. His hair was now very long and gray and so was his beard. He lived with his mother and did nothing. And he never entered the building.

I cannot simply go home at night. I remember as a child in Chicago riding in the back seat of beat-up old cars and peering at the bad neighborhoods. A curtain or drape would be hanging out a second-story window, a long tongue of cloth beating against the dirty bricks of a tenement, and the faces would stare impassively, the streets would be littered, and here and there boards would stand duty where glass had failed. World War II had ended and this is what we had won. Everything would be gray: the walls, the streets, the faces, the sky, the past, the present, the future. I would think, how can this exist? Why doesn't someone do something? How can we simply go home and have our dinner and never mention any of this? These questions, of course, were childish.

Now I am no longer a child and I seldom admit to thinking such things. I visit many rooms, I make notes on pieces of paper or in my mind, and then I go away. I would like to think that part of what keeps me moving can be found in the back seat of beat-up old cars sliding through the bad neighborhoods and the broken faces. But I am not sure.

A year after Nacho's death, a Mexican is indicted for the killing. The man has the usual past. A few years before, the alleged killer's father had disappointed someone. So his legs were chained to separate automobiles and then he was torn apart. A friend tells me this over a beer. Anna is out of jail again. Lupita continues to survive in the life. The summer heat smothers conversation.

A man comes to my house and says, there is this village in Mexico you must visit where they raise marijuana, a place where Anglos are not allowed to go. He says, I will take you there. I have just finished a story on a bankrupt local businessman, a brief flame in the blaze of American greed. The businessman's office is fine wood, marble, brass fittings, a view that rolls out endlessly from the top of a glass tower. He is Mexican American but speaks no Spanish and does not go to Mexico. He tells me there are many opportunities in the market right now if one knows what to buy and when to sell. He is ready for more action, he says.

I think of the offer to take me into the village.

Some things simply are.

Some things are not being reported.

A friend drops by, she has been working in L.A. The

project has been vast, intricate, and profitable. She is very skilled. Sometimes she runs loads for the money, but she is backing off this. The calls from friends in jail give her pause. One night she came home and found a few hundred pounds on her living-room floor. This, she did not like. Her friend asked, "What's wrong? I just need a place to stash it for a day or two." So she began looking for quieter work.

The project in L.A., she tells me, was for a kind of amusement center in Japan. Americans are building it because they have more imagination, and because their labor is much cheaper. There will be seven rooms, and you will enter this maze carrying a laser gun. She designed the armament. The first room will look like a command center with robots tending the screens, twirling dials at the huge console. Then, without warning, the robots will begin firing, the console will open up with more firepower, walls will slide open, and yet more guns will draw down on you. This continues through seven rooms, chambers where light fixtures, house plants, tasteful objects will suddenly flower like weeds and blaze away at you. You have one hundred shots and there are fifty things seeking to kill you. So you must be careful, you must not wallow in your killing but be surgical. The charge for this adventure is ten or twenty bucks American. The Japanese, she assures me, will love it. They are so repressed, she explains, they need a place to play at killing.

The whole maze was assembled in L.A. in pieces so it could be shipped and reassembled. It is very high tech, the designers and builders are all special effects people from the film industry. Everyone is being flown over for the final construction. One guy that worked on the thing was a *cholo*, a gang member from East L.A., the arms covered with tattoos, the total badass thing. Christ, he was trouble before they got there, getting drunk on the plane and raising hell. And then when they landed and checked through

customs, the Japanese officials found he had a big pig
sticker strapped to his body. No one can carry a blade like
that in Japan, it is a peaceful country, so they demanded
the knife. The *cholo* would not surrender it. He's from
East L.A., you know. So they shipped him and he lost his
job.

If the maze is a hit, they figure to build fifty more in
Japan. People can't get enough of this laser gun killing.

We walk toward town. There are sea shell fragments scattered among the stones and soon we reach the shore. The
fish are dying, good-sized fish, and in the shallow water I
can see hundreds of them flopping in their death throes. It
is the temperature, the water has become too cool for their
needs, they are a specialty breed imported from Egypt. So
they perish. The shore is lined with large campers and old
people sit outside and drink beer and talk while the fish
flop and die. Further on we enter a thicket bordering a
marsh. Dozens of little herons rise up from the reeds and
flap their wings slowly. They seem intense with life. The
odor of dead fish thickens like a paste in the air.

My eyes quicken at the sight of the birds. The long beaks
and necks seem keen for every moment of the day.

I no longer wonder why I go.

I wonder why I come back at all. And why others never
go at all. I have stopped thinking about the miles, the
booze, the women. Actually, I have never thought about
such matters. They are categories others bring to my attention during various lectures on behavior and then to
please them I fabricate answers.

I no longer wonder why I go.

I go.

I drive to Phoenix. The man waits in a room. There is a
great deal of noise, voices crackling through intercoms,
doors banging. He is shackled at his waist and feet. The

face is pleasant, almost professorial. He has spent nine years on Death Row and wishes to talk. In a day or two, another man will confess in open court to the crime—beating a man to death with a frying pan and then strangling the victim with his own necktie. Because of this turn of events, the man I am speaking to will then have a good shot at freedom.

He has spent twenty-five years in the joint and we talk for hours about his life and his many crimes. He has always been a thief. Not a very good one, but a dedicated one. He is very intelligent, a member of MENSA with a I.Q. of 160 or more. We talk for two days. He is very proud of his intellect and often speaks like a sociology professor, the language clotted with jargon and structured to deny any connection between emotion and human thought. When he talks of cooking on Death Row, of smuggling in a small stove, stockpiling rare spices, whipping up omelettes, his tongue suddenly comes alive and living sentences pour out.

He tells me that when he gets out, he has arranged to have someone with him for at least a year. This person will walk with him and stay by his side. This is necessary, he tells me, because he has trained reflexes from his years in prison. If you hesitate for just a second in the joint, he laughs, you've already got three holes in your chest. I know I will edit the laughter out of his remarks. No one will understand that laughter who is not sitting in this cell. He repeats that he will need a buffer between himself and the world. At least for a while, he figures. Until he forgets what he has learned. He is balding and wears thin spectacles like a college professor. Once while escaping the police, he shot a man. He tells me he fled to his home and then vomited. I ask him why? Because, he says with a flash of intensity, I realized I could have gotten hurt.

That night I sit in a bar and watch a blind singer. Her jeans are skintight, she is about thirty, and very lovely. She

plays to an audience she cannot see. I wonder how she can
sense the crowd's reactions or if she can sense them. The tables are full of businessmen with other businessmen and men with women and they are all drinking and talking. Their faces are pasty and soft and their fingers have thin gold rings. Sometimes they glance over at the blind singer, but usually they do not. She is being ignored. Does she know this? I watch her all night.

When the show is over, her mother comes out of the crowd and helps her down from the tiny stage. I am sitting with a woman and we watch this evening of sightless singing take place. I put down my drink and marvel at the fact that the woman is blind, and so lovely, and so willing to send her voice into a room her eyes cannot scan.

The woman sitting with me pauses and says, "How do you know she is blind?"

Finally during that last night, the cat relaxed. I could feel the tension and fear leave her body like a soul wandering off on some mission. The breathing grew more steady, but still I was reluctant to move. And so I lay there with the cat pressed against my face, the moisture seeping from the ruined nose onto my cheek. I did not turn on the television with the remote control box or flip on the light. There were only two sounds: boxcars switching from train to train in the yard a mile away, and the soft flutter of her breath as she drank sleep deeply and with abandon.

In the morning, she slid off my chest and went about her business. It is the night that brings the fear, I think.

We reach the town after seven miles of slogging. In the air, we moved at one hundred fifty miles an hour, now we move at two or three. We laugh about this change in velocity but can make little sense of it. It simply is, a curious fact to toss back and forth at each other. The community is based on retired people who were expected to come and buy little lots and throw up cheap houses. There is a yacht club with a bar and restaurant and a marina with no boats moored. But out on the water is the hope of fish, of the long cast and the hard strike, of the stringer heavy with the catch to prove time has passed and been used properly and turned to account. Now the fish have been declared poisoned by some agency and people are warned not to eat them too often. This has not created prosperity.

The town is failing, the businesses all largely gone bust and left to cobwebs. A black man works at an abandoned gas station. There is a big hole in the ground where a new fuel tank will be buried, and next door is a closed grocery he is committed to reopening. He has lived on the coast but now is moved inland to try his luck and seize the main chance. He speaks flatly of his problems and voices no complaint. The air sags with the stench of the dead fish. It will work out, he says, he is willing to make the effort.

I think: there is always a beginning in each end.

We find an open café and eat fried shrimp and talk to the waitress. The ceiling is acoustical tile and she has painted every other square a pink. She says it makes the ceiling seem lower and more cosy. It took her whole vacation to do it, there are five hundred pink tiles staring down at us.

I feel very relaxed and find it difficult to speak. I no longer hear the cat struggling to breathe. And the woman tells me of aircraft and their oddities and quirks and why she flies.

"It's to be alone," she says.

The night comes softly and then cold slams down from the mountains. The moon floods the sky and drives the stars away. About two in the morning it finally sinks, a gold disk, and the constellations emerge and dance across the heavens.

We sleep next to the plane's wing. Once, an owl hoots. Later, a coyote yelps. The woman tells me that she has

been trying to think of a way to state what really matters.
She thinks spirit sums up what really matters. She knows
it is not intelligence, she has met too many bright people
with dim lives. So it must be spirit, the ability to embrace
whatever is delivered.

Her hair smells clean and the airplane stands against
the night sky as an outline of order. Soon I will find it
difficult to recall the rasping breath of the cat on the last
night. A kitten will appear. They always do. The high
school reunions will have light and laughter and a darkness at the edge of the parking lot.

I am at ease. With the night.

I lie there and write the names of rivers on a pad. I want
to think of tumbling water and living things and strands of
desire coursing across the land.

In the morning, the woman says she is happy because I
did not seem disturbed that she was the pilot and I was the
baggage. She says many men have problems with a
woman in control.

I return to the straitjacket of conversation. It is the ap-
propriate thing to do.

It is another night, another place. We meet for a drink.
The hair is long and dark, the eyes open and friendly, and
she is leaning forward. She wishes to explain something to
me. I can barely hear through the taped rock-'n'-roll
music, but the message comes through.

Each New Year's Eve she gets in her plane and goes up
into the night sky over the city. Down below people are
drinking together and eyeing each other and puzzling out
the failures of the past year and their hopes for the next
year. This she avoids. In the airplane, she is all alone, not
even she is there, she tells me. She stops thinking and simply is.

I look into her face with some amazement. She is tall,
the boots underscoring her height, and she has the ges-

tures—the fingers brushing my sleeve, the sparkle in the eyes, the soft lilt of her words—of a woman who does not hunger for dark rooms, sad poems, and lonely hours. There is the child, the broken marriage, the list of odd jobs, the dancing for money in the clubs, the other states and odd venues she has spent time in. She is my age and we are all the same.

She keeps speaking.

Once she is up, she goes for the searchlights. They are out every New Year's Eve, she brightens. She does not know why or who exactly beams them into the sky. Perhaps the resorts? Or some swank supper clubs? She has never checked the matter out. It does not concern her. The lights, she wants me to know, keep rotating across the sky and she aims for the beam. This is not a simple matter. She must calculate where the brilliant shaft will lance her altitude when it swings past. And airplanes, she smiles, have no reverse. She must hit it right or she absolutely misses.

I drain my wine and listen with apparent hunger. She finishes her tale and smiles broadly.

She never tells me if she has hit the beam.

I never ask.

A white cat has appeared in the yard. The head is large, the animal is an uncut male. He does not come near yet, but watches with eyes of knowing and glances of studied contempt. He has found vacant territory and seized the ground. The birds appear indifferent, they live on a planet where cats are everywhere. The white cat moves slowly and with stated grace.

I am looking at maps now. There is the Blue River country, a fifty-mile slog into the former haunt of grizzly bears and wolves. I want to speak to their ghosts. I sense this is possible, I think this is absurd. And then the lower reaches of the Little Colorado to the salt lick of the Hopis and the point where life emerged from the lower world. In the smoky air of their kivas, the tribesmen insist this is the true account. I am willing.

I am sitting on the terrace of a local racquet club, drinking and watching the mountains grab shadows from the afternoon sky. A friend considers my various wanderings and says the trouble is that I have no quest, no beginning, middle, and end. No Holy Grail. He says such a structure is essential for any story. The terrace is filled with hard bodies determined to look pleasing and healthy and tan. I drain my glass of wine.

I think that perhaps we just see the world differently. That for me the end means the beginning was false, the entire march an errand to the grocery store.

The women on the terrace look especially good with that glow that comes after a work-out and shower. Their skin is an irresistible meal.

I tell him of the woman who hunts the searchlights each New Year's Eve and he sighs and says that I don't understand, that it matters if she hits the beams, that I should ask and find out the answer.

But it does not matter.

I have already left town.

I am sitting in a bar, a place paneled with wood, dimly lit for fantasy. I have a very strong desire to drive a very long distance and drive that distance very fast. My truck does not even have a tachometer. I will have to guess where the edge is this time. I want to get in the machine—it will be parked inside this fine hotel bar. I will start the engine, let it warm up a bit, and put the right tape in the cassette deck. Then I will floor the pedal and tear through the wood and glass walls, shards flashing through the saloon air, all the sharp and surprising edges gleaming. And I will be outside and moving into the night.

Its bite is harmful....
It is a persevering revenger of injuries.... And it
may avenge an injury and exact a penalty from

some troublesome man by finding out his dwelling place with great perseverance and care, and killing some of his domestic animals. But it is grateful to those who do well by it. . . .
            —first printed description of a coyote in
                Francisco Hernandez, Nova Plantarum,
                Animalium et Mineralium
                Mexicanorum Historia, 1651

ACKNOWLEDGMENTS

I want to thank my friend Arturo Carrillo Strong for going with me into some odd places and leading me into some odder ones. He never stopped arguing with me—a gift of great value. He is a good man to have in a bad place. He also is curious, a trait most people claim and very few practice.

Some of the material in this book has appeared, in earlier disguises, in the *Journal of the Southwest, City Magazine,* the Tucson *Citizen,* and the San Francisco *Examiner.* David McCumber and Will Hearst of the *Examiner* put up with my vague ideas and bad habits and I am grateful for their tolerance. I want to thank the people who were kind enough to read various versions of the manuscript, particularly Alan Harrington, who wields a sharp blue pencil. I also want to thank Ed Abbey, who never read the manuscript, he just insisted I get it published and helped me find a way.

Julian Hayden never asked me what I was doing, or stopped pouring shots of mezcal. And I needed that.